A PUCKING WRONG
CHRISTMAS

THE PUCKING WRONG SERIES

A PUCKING WRONG CHRISTMAS

A PUCKING WRONG NOVELLA

DALLAS
KNIGHTS

C.R. JANE

Cover design by Cassie Chapman/Opulent Designs

ISBN: 978-1-0394-8650-8

Published in 2024 by Podium Publishing
www.podiumentertainment.com

Podium

To all my red flag renegades who made it onto the Naughty List this year.

My Dear Red Flag Renegades,

The holidays can be complicated. Whether we're disappointed by current festivities that don't meet our expectations or haunted by the ghosts of Christmases past, what is supposed to be the happiest, jolliest time of year . . . sometimes isn't quite what we'd hoped for.

With our reigning queen of the circle of trust, Monroe, I knew there was a holiday story to tell. Given her tragic background and the painful memories that come from having a mother who battled addiction, she has feelings on the subject, to say the least.

Monroe may seem innocent—maybe even naïve—on the surface, but she has an inner strength that I love. The ability to come back and, dare I say, thrive after such a hard childhood is my favorite thing about her. And Lincoln's obsession with making her happy, well, that could be my favorite thing about him.

The circle of trust is growing, and writing these crazy, red-flag men is the most fun I've ever had as an author. Ari Lancaster continues to dominate my brain, and the text chains in this book usually start with some off-the-wall thing he's said to the group. As Ari would say, he's the gift that keeps on giving.

One of my favorite parts about this series is the idea of found family—that even with tragic or disappointing pasts, we can find a network of people who love and support us no matter what. Blake is always going to have some demons; Monroe is always going to have her childhood hovering in the back of her mind. But their support system is going to get them through the hard times . . . always.

A Pucking Wrong Christmas is a spicy, sweet taste of the holidays, and I hope you love revisiting these characters as much as I enjoyed writing them!

A PUCKING WRONG CHRISTMAS *PLAYLIST*

CHRISTMAS TREE FARM
Taylor Swift

TIS THE DAMN SEASON
Taylor Swift

WINTERSONG
Sarah McLachlan

SANTA CLAUS IS COMING TO TOWN
Frank Sinatra

SANTA CLAUS IS COMING TO TOWN
Mariah Carey

WE WISH YOU A MERRY CHRISTMAS
Pentatonix

RUN RUDOLPH RUN
Chuck Berry

JINGLE BELL ROCK
Bobby Helms

SCAN CODE TO LISTEN ON SPOTIFY

WARNING

Dear readers, this is a novella set in Ari Lancaster's book, *The Pucking Wrong Guy*. There are small spoilers for *The Pucking Wrong Number* and *The Pucking Wrong Guy*, but in my opinion, it can still be read on its own. It is best enjoyed however, after you have met Lincoln and Ari.

Prepare to enter the world of the Dallas Knights . . . you've been warned.

A PUCKING WRONG CHRISTMAS

PROLOGUE
MONROE

Four Years Old . . .

It was the most exciting night ever! I sat on the floor, surrounded by boxes of shiny stuff, while Mom held a string of twinkly lights. Our apartment smelled like yummy cookies, and there was music playing in the background that made me feel all warm inside.

Mom smiled at me and gave me a glass thingy with a pretty angel on it. "Here, sweetie, let's put this one first. It was your grandma's favorite."

I held the glass thingy real careful in my little hands. The angel had golden wings and was so pretty. "It's so, so pretty, Mommy!"

We hung the angel on a branch, and it twinkled with the lights all around it. I felt like it was a magic angel, just like the ones in my storybooks.

Mom told me stories about when she was a little kid, like me, and how she used to wake up super early on Christmas morning. She talked about opening presents and being with her family, and her eyes sparkled when she talked about it. It was like she was telling me a bedtime story, but it was real.

Mom was different tonight. Her eyes were alert and she was speaking to me so nice. It made me think that maybe that story I had read at school last week was right—that miracles did happen on Christmas.

"I wish every day could be like Christmas," I whispered.

Mom looked at me and smiled real soft. "I promise, sweetheart. I'm gonna be right here with you, and we're gonna have the best Christmas ever."

I felt all warm and fuzzy inside, like I was wrapped in a cozy blanket. Putting shiny things on the tree felt like a magical adventure with Mom, just like the stories in my books.

When we put the last shiny thing—the ornament she'd told me it was called—on the tree, I was so happy. The room was all sparkly from the lights on the tree, and it smelled like cookies. Mom said she loved me more than anything, and I said I loved her too.

We sat together by the tree, and it felt like the best Christmas ever. It wasn't just about the shiny things or the lights; it was about Mommy and me being together and feeling all warm and happy inside on Christmas Eve.

After we finished decorating the Christmas tree, Mom smiled down at me and said, "Alright, sweetie, it's time for bed. Santa will be here soon."

I looked up at her with wide, hopeful eyes. "Is Santa really coming, Mommy? Sometimes he forgets."

Her eyes dimmed and for a moment I felt panicked. I didn't want to make Mommy sad tonight. She got bad again when she was sad.

"But I don't mind, Mommy. Honest, I don't!"

Mom bent down and kissed my forehead. "He won't forget this time, Monroe. You've been such a good girl this year, and Santa knows it. He's going to bring you the most wonderful presents."

I couldn't help but grin at the thought of Santa coming with presents just for me. I nodded eagerly. "Okay, Mommy, I'll go to bed."

Mom tucked me in, making sure the blankets were snug around me. "Now, remember, sweetie, you have to stay in bed and go to sleep. Santa won't come if you're awake."

I nodded again, determined to be the best little girl ever. "I'll stay in bed, Mommy, I promise."

Mom leaned down and gave me one last kiss. "Goodnight, Monroe. Sweet dreams, and I'll see you in the morning."

With that, she turned off the bedroom light and closed the door behind her.

I closed my eyes, feeling the excitement bubbling inside me. Santa was on his way. He wasn't going to forget. She had promised.

I settled into bed, determined to be fast asleep before Santa's arrival.

I woke up with my heart all jumpy and wiggly, like there were butterflies inside my tummy. Christmas was finally here! I yanked my blanket off of me and jumped out of bed, ready to race to the living room.

Through the door, I could hear Christmas music playing softly and I grinned. Mommy was probably already up and ready for the best day ever. I couldn't wait to see what Santa brought me.

I pushed open the door and ran into the room, all ready to see the magic.

But the magic wasn't there.

Our Christmas tree, which was supposed to be all pretty and twinkly, was on the floor. All the shiny ornaments were broken into pieces, and the tinsel was everywhere.

I walked over and stared at the tree, freezing when I saw it— the angel ornament that Mommy had told me was her mommy's favorite. It was broken into pieces on the ground.

I reached down and picked up the broken angel. My eyes got

watery, and my bottom lip wobbled. This wasn't what I thought I'd see on Christmas morning. I looked over at Mommy, who was all curled up on the couch with bottles all around her. She looked sleepy and messy.

"Mom?" I whispered, going closer. "Mommy, wake up!"

But Mommy didn't wake up. She just made a funny noise and kept sleeping. I looked down at all the broken, shiny things, and it felt like the tears in my eyes were gonna spill out like rain.

"Mommy, where's Santa?" I asked, my voice all shaky. "Where are our presents?"

Mommy blinked her eyes open, and she looked all tired and confused. "Monroe?" she said, like she didn't really know me. "What are you doing up so early, sweetie?"

I pointed at our poor Christmas tree and all the mess. "Look, Mommy! Our tree is all broken, and there's no presents."

Mommy tried to sit up, but she wobbled like a sleepy jellybean. "I . . . I don't know, Monroe," she said, and her words were all mixed up. "I thought I could . . . I thought I could make it special for you. But Christmas is so hard . . . "

I couldn't stop the tears now, and they came pouring down like rain on a stormy day. I plopped down on the floor, and it felt like my heart was crying too.

"I thought I'd been good for Santa," I sniffled, my voice full of sadness.

Mommy reached out and pulled me into her arms, and I buried my face in her shoulder. She smelled like Mommy, and even though everything was all messy, I felt safe in her arms.

"I'm so sorry, Monroe," she whispered, and her voice was soft and sad. "I messed up, baby. I messed up bad."

I found out later, in a drunken confession, Mom had sold all of the presents that a "Secret Santa" had given us to chase another high.

And I'd hated Christmas ever since.

CHAPTER 1
MONROE

NOW

"Oh the weather outside is frightful . . . " Christmas music cut through the cozy silence of my sleep and I blearily opened my eyes, searching for the offensive song.

"Good morning, baby," Lincoln purred, suddenly hovering over me.

His beauty stunned me for a second, as it did every time I saw him. It was enough to push the song out of my head. Whenever he was near, he was all I could see.

"Hi," I whispered, reaching up to touch his cheek. He pushed into my touch, that awestruck look in his eyes that he always had around me, like I was the prize and he couldn't believe how lucky he was to have me.

He was out of his mind.

But I guess I already knew that . . .

And so was I.

"It's December 1st," he said as he leaned forward and pulled down the sheet covering my chest. My nipples pebbled as the cold air hit them.

"Mmmh, is it?" I asked, my voice breathy.

"My favorite time of year," he continued as his lips trailed along my neck, kissing and licking.

I moaned as his hands began to knead my breasts.

"For some reason, I thought Halloween was your favorite." Lincoln lifted his head up to stare at me with those golden eyes of his. Amused. Very amused.

"And why's that?" he asked innocently before he suddenly bit down on my nipple, making me writhe on the bed.

"Because you're kind of a psycho."

"A psycho, huh?" he asked, moving his mouth to my other breast.

"Definitely."

His hand slipped between my legs, probing into my sex and attacking my sensitive bundle of nerves.

I was panting, whimpers steadily flowing out of my mouth.

He thrust his fingers in and out as my eyes closed and I grabbed onto his broad shoulders as an orgasm began to build.

Lincoln licked and kissed along my pulse. "I'm pretty sure you like that I'm a psycho, dream girl," he growled.

"Hmmm . . . I'm not sure about that."

His growl deepened this time, and he thrust another finger inside me, making me squeal.

Lincoln abruptly pulled his fingers out of me and pushed my legs apart, shoving them wide. A second later his mouth was on my clit, and he was sucking and licking feverishly. His amber gaze stared at me with a dark, possessive look. "You like how crazy I am about you, baby." His tongue slowly slid through my folds. "You like that I have to begin and end my days in your sweet pussy. That I can't concentrate on anything else. That all I think about is how much I want you, need you, fucking love you." He shoved my legs up to my shoulders, his mouth closing over my clit once more, sucking on it . . . hard. I squirmed against his face but his arms were across my hips, holding me down. His tongue fucked inside my pussy, and he moaned as if it was the best thing he'd ever tasted.

Knowing Lincoln, he probably did think that.

And I was perfectly okay with it.

The sounds coming out of his mouth were erotic and raw, and I was gushing all over his face.

"Fuck. That's so good. You're so fucking sweet." His tongue slid through my folds, circling my clit before sliding back to plunge into my core. The sounds of his mouth on me, his pants as he thrust into me, his breath against my skin . . . how he hit that perfect spot every time. My insides wound tighter and then . . . everything inside me clenched violently as an orgasm shot through me.

Lincoln was a man possessed as he continued to devour me, licking and sucking like he was desperate to get every drop.

When I was so sensitive it was almost painful, he abruptly pulled back, angled his hips, and forced his thick cock into my still clenching core. A thrill ran through me as I saw the last of my name disappearing inside me, a mark he carried with him everywhere, right along with the ring on his finger that he refused to ever take off.

"There's nothing that feels as good as this. You fucking take me so fucking well." He arched back displaying his perfect, straining muscles. His abs flexed as he moved, and I felt a little dazed as I stared at the tensed muscles in his neck. I've never seen anything more beautiful in my entire life. And he was all mine.

"Lincoln," I moaned as he pushed deeper inside me. No matter how many times he took me—and it was constantly—it was always a tight fit. Like now, as he forced that last inch inside of me, making me feel whole in only the way that he could . . . only the way that he *would*.

"Good girl," he whispered as he settled on top of me. The words spread through my insides, warming me with pleasure, just like they always did.

"Look at me," Lincoln demanded, and my gaze shot to his dark and possessive stare. His fingers dug into my hips, every thrust hitting that perfect spot inside me.

My pussy pulsed around his thick length and a wave of pleasure laced through me. My breath was coming out in ragged gasps.

"Baby, that's right. Squeeze my dick."

"Lincoln, please," I whimpered as he slammed in and out of me.

"Tell me that you love that I'm a psycho for you," he suddenly demanded, sliding out of me slowly, a sensuous pace that threatened to do me in. My gaze slipped to his cock, glistening with our combined wetness. Lincoln slid his hand between us, sliding his fingers over his dick and bringing them up to my lips. I immediately opened, sucking every drop and moaning as I did so. This might be a game that I liked to play to drive him over the edge, but we both knew that he owned me.

Body and soul.

There wasn't anything about Lincoln Daniels that I wasn't crazy about anymore. Hence why I considered myself a crazy person too.

"Are you going to say it?" he asked after he pulled his fingers from my mouth. "Or do I have to stop?"

"No! Don't stop," I pleaded and he laughed wickedly, running his thumb across my bottom lip.

"Then say it, Monroe. Give me what I want." Each word was punctuated by a staccato thrust that wasn't enough to get me what I wanted.

"Please," I gasped as he bit down on the slope of my breast before licking the pain away.

"Say it," he whispered.

"I love you, you crazy fucking psycho," I growled as I thrashed underneath him.

His answering smile took my breath away, and my pussy flooded and clenched around his cock.

"Good girl," he murmured as he pulled back and slammed back in, *finally* giving me the pace that I was desperate for.

"Is that what you needed, sweetheart?" he murmured. "My big dick inside your pretty pussy?"

"Yes, Yes, Yes," I chanted as his body worked above me. I devoured the sight of his muscles flexing.

My orgasm was building, sharp pleasure already sliding across my skin in anticipation.

"Who do you belong to?" he growled as he angled his hips, plunging into me in long, deep strokes.

"You," I told him, unable to play games anymore.

"That's right. Only me. You're mine."

I fell into a spiraling, devastating orgasm that had the edges of my vision darkening because it was so freaking intense. His possessiveness and dark devotion were everything to me.

He was everything to me.

Lincoln Daniels owned me, body and soul.

"I love you, I love you so fucking much," he murmured as his hips rolled into me, sending smaller orgasms sparking through me.

"I love you too," I gasped as I watched in a lust-filled daze as he chased his orgasm, his body finally going rigid as his cock pulsed inside me, filling me with his hot cum in bursts until I was overflowing with *him* . . . just like I always wanted.

His large frame collapsed on top of me, covering me with his perfect warmth.

"I wish I could live inside of you," he murmured.

"I'm pretty sure you do," I huffed faintly. He stroked my cheek softly before nuzzling into my hair.

"Yeah, you're right."

It felt like too much, this thing between us, a living, breathing, overpowering beast that overtook everything else.

Just then, the fact that Christmas music was still playing filtered into my consciousness.

"Can you turn that off?" I asked with a sigh.

His forehead crinkled in confusion. "Turn what off?"

"The music."

"Not a fan of the Biebs? 'Mistletoe' is a classic!"

"Not a fan of Christmas actually."

Lincoln gaped down at me.

———

Lincoln

I stared down at my beautiful girl, my cock still buried deep inside of her. What had she just said? And why didn't I know that about her? I thought I knew everything about Monroe at this point. I'd made it my mission in life—to find out everything so that I could make her life the best it could possibly be.

But maybe I'd just assumed . . .

Immediate hatred spiked through my gut because I knew it had something to do with the worthless piece of shit that was her mother. Maybe you shouldn't think ill of the dead, but I'd have a lot to say to that woman if she was alive right now. She deserved all the pain and misery she'd had in her life.

I rolled us over so that I was on my back and she was sprawled across me. My dick was hard again, but I was used to ignoring it at this point. If I fucked her as often as I wanted, her pussy would probably break.

And we couldn't have that. I loved it too much.

"Tell me," I demanded, hating the look of defeat in her gaze.

She tried to look away and I thrust up so that I had her attention once again.

Monroe sighed and rolled her eyes. "Do I have to tell you everything?"

"Yes," I replied simply. "That's how this works. You tell me what hurts. And I make it better."

Her features softened and I held in my groan. Because when she looked at me like that . . . it was hard not to fuck her. Immediately.

"Just a bad Christmas when I was a kid. She made promises. Broke them. And Santa never came. Kind of scarring as a little kid," she whispered. "It happened a bunch of times but for some reason *that* Christmas was what broke me."

I groaned and brushed a kiss against her lips, licking up the tear that had fallen down her face.

"I hate that I can't erase every single one of those bad memories, baby," I murmured, surging up into her.

She gasped and grasped my face, brushing her own gentle kiss across my lips. "You make everything else better though," she whispered. My fingers dug into her hips and I pushed up into her again.

Sometimes . . . a lot of times . . . words weren't enough with this girl. I couldn't adequately tell her why my soul lived inside her. Why I was obsessed with everything about her.

My words weren't enough to make her feel this *need* inside of me.

But my body sure as fuck could.

CHAPTER 2
LINCOLN

An hour later, I'd finally let her out of bed and she was seated at the counter while I made breakfast.

"So how far does this hatred of Christmas go? Are Christmas pancakes allowed?" I asked casually.

She cocked her head, biting down on her lip in a way that made my dick twitch despite the fact that I'd cum several times this morning already.

"Christmas pancakes . . . what are those?"

"Let me surprise you," I told her, an idea forming. I had a shitty upbringing with my psycho parents. But there was the one time of year when my family always pulled their shit together before my brother died . . . Christmas. It was the only time where my mom acted like a mom. Where my dad wasn't the consummate asshole. And after my brother died . . . I had Ari.

Since one of my goals was to replace all of Monroe's bad memories with good ones, Christmas seemed like a good one to add to the list.

I couldn't cook for shit, but Mrs. Bentley had left us the batter for her famous Christmas pancakes, a tradition we'd had for years. I could handle those at least.

Thirty minutes later, the pancakes were done. Buttery, coconut perfection if I didn't fucking say so myself with whipped cream, macadamia nuts, and coconut syrup. I set the plate down in front of Monroe with a flourish before lifting her up and settling down in the chair with her in my lap. She squirmed and I sighed. Another breakfast with an erection pushing against her ass.

She glanced back at me over her shoulder with a smirk, and I growled.

"Eat your damn breakfast, pretty girl."

I scooped up a bite of the pancakes, making sure to get one loaded with all the toppings, and I held it up to her lips.

She opened like the fucking good girl she was and let me feed her the bite.

"Holy crap," she murmured after a moment. "I think that's the best thing I've ever tasted."

I bit down gently on her neck, thinking that covering her in that coconut syrup would be better.

"Christmas pancakes," I murmured.

"Just pancakes," she corrected, opening her mouth for another bite.

"Christmas pancakes, baby. And you love them, so that's one point in the 'Christmas is great' column."

She huffed, but there was a small smile on her lips right before I fed her another bite.

My plan was officially in action.

I'd dropped Monroe off for her class and I was sitting in the arena parking lot, about to go in for weights, when my phone buzzed.

It was Ari, of course. And Walker.

Ari: December 1st fools. It's xmas time.

Me: We have a problem.

Walker: What do you need!?

I snorted at Walker's eagerness.

Ari: Aww Disney. Such a cute simp.

Disney:

Ari: But if Golden Boy has a problem, I will be the one solving it. Bestie privileges.

Me: Focus.

Ari: Sir, yes, sir.

Walker: He's eye-rolling at you so hard right now.

Idiots. Both of them. And the best fucking guys I knew.

Me: Monroe hates Christmas.

Ari: WHAT DID YOU JUST SAY?

Walker: Um . . . sorry about that?

Me: Don't worry, I'm going to change her mind . . . but any ideas you boys have . . .

Walker: I'll send over a list!

Ari: OMG, Walker. I will send over a list.

Shaking my head, I ignored them to check my tracking app and make sure Monroe was in class where she was supposed to be. Assured she was where I'd left her, I tossed my phone into my bag and headed inside to work out.

My phone buzzed the entire walk inside as Ari and Walker both sent me idea after idea of how to make Monroe like Christmas.

CHAPTER 3

BLAKE

The sand was soft and warm beneath my bare feet, and a gentle breeze kissed my skin, carrying the scent of saltwater and tropical blooms. The sun hung low in the sky, casting a warm, golden glow across the horizon.

I walked towards the water, drawn by the rhythmic melody of the waves. Each step felt like a caress from the earth itself, a soothing balm to my soul. The turquoise waters stretched out before me, their depths inviting and mysterious.

As I approached the shoreline, I dipped my toes into the crystal clear water. It was refreshingly cool, sending a shiver of delight up my spine. The sensation was invigorating, like a gentle reminder that I was alive and free in this dreamlike paradise.

With every step, I waded deeper into the cerulean embrace of the sea. The water lapped at my ankles, then my knees, as I continued to walk further in. The water began to take form, sliding up my legs in soft licks, kissing and tasting my skin as it slid up my thighs. My legs pushed apart as I fell back into the waves, letting the water cradle me as it rushed over my core, sucking on my clit as it pressed inside me, my insides immediately tightening as pleasure washed through me. And then . . .

"Good morning, sunshine," a familiar voice said, amused.

My eyes flew open and I realized I was in fact, not in Fiji . . . I was in Ari's—our—place, with my gorgeous dark-haired boyfriend in between my legs, his tongue slowly licking through my folds as he watched me with heavy-lidded eyes.

"Hi," I whimpered as he ate into me, licking me everywhere, including the cove of my ass as I wiggled against him. His mouth went to my clit, sucking hard as his fingers caressed me.

"Come for me and I'll give you a surprise," he said roughly as his tongue replaced his fingers inside me, his nose pressing against my clit as he rubbed that perfect place . . .

"Ari," I cried as an orgasm ripped through me, surprising me with its intensity as I ground my core against his face.

I was panting as I came down from my high, my hands tangled in Ari's hair as he chuckled against my skin, giving me a few more licks for good measure.

"Delicious," he growled as he lifted his head and prowled up my body. "Ready for your surprise?"

"I think the orgasm before breakfast was good enough."

"Now, sunshine, you know I always like to be an over-achiever."

Something hard slid against me and I glanced down . . . because it didn't feel like it was his dick.

My eyes widened as I stared down at what was sitting between us, sheathing his dick completely.

It was a present. His dick was wrapped in a present. A large present. Complete with a red bow.

"What the fuck—"

"It's my dick in a box," he said in a completely serious voice. "Want to unwrap it?" He jostled the box for good measure and I could hear his dick smacking the sides of the box as he moved.

We stared at each other for a long moment before I burst into giggles, my head thrown back against the pillow as I laughed so hard I started crying.

Ari slid off me and rolled to my side. He propped his head up on one sexy, muscled arm and shook his head at me in mock sadness. "Laughing at my gift to you. I can't believe it."

"Have you been wanting to do that since you saw that SNL skit?" I barked out in between laughs.

He sighed. "You haven't seen most of the greatest movies of all time . . . and yet somehow you've seen the 'Dick in a Box' skit. Why am I not surprised?"

"I'm sorry," I snorted, dragging my finger down his chest until it was hovering right above the box. It was a big box . . . but I was pretty sure he still had to stuff his dick inside of it to fit.

My man was a beast.

"I think you should unwrap your present to make me feel better since you've been laughing at my gift for ten minutes," Ari pouted, his muscles flexing as he brushed some of his dark hair out of his face.

I pretended to think about it and then finally reached forward to grab the red ribbon. "That's probably the polite thing to do," I said in a serious voice.

I pulled on the ribbon, watching as his tongue peeked out and he slowly licked along his bottom lip.

My personal kryptonite when it came to him.

I was achy inside, need growing as we played, despite the fact that he'd just given me an orgasm.

The ribbon untied easily and I lifted the lid, another laugh slipping out of my lips when I saw his pierced dick stuffed inside the box, courtesy of a hole he'd carved into the side of the box.

"I can't believe this is happening," I snorted.

Ari thrust his hips forward. "You *are* that lucky, sweetheart."

I carefully pulled the box away from his dick and tossed it behind me.

"Mmmhh," Ari choked, as I bent forward and licked the tip of his cock. "Does that mean you like my gift?"

"Best gift ever," I told him. "Now get on the bed. I want to enjoy my present."

His eyes lit up and he bounced onto the bed eagerly, flopping onto his back while his massive dick stood at attention.

I leaned over his body and pressed a kiss on his chest, my tongue dipping out to taste his smooth skin.

"Fuck, sunshine. I love you," he breathed.

The words sent warmth flooding through my veins.

I made my way down his chest, licking and kissing my way across his chiseled abdomen.

He trembled under my lips, his sharp inhale turning me on. I loved that I could affect him like that. This gorgeous, perfect man. I could make him desperate for me.

I intended to do just that.

"Blake, please," he begged, and I smiled at him before leaning down and licking up his shaft, keeping eye contact with him the entire time.

"Do you like teasing me, baby?" He reached down and played with a strand of my hair. "Because I'm not sure how long I can play like this . . . "

"Before what?" I asked innocently, again licking along his length.

The musky smell of him was making my mouth water.

I ran my fingertips along his cock, tracing the veins along his pierced skin before I brushed against the rim of his head. There was a bead of precum along his slit and I licked it off, moaning at the taste.

I'd never get enough of him.

His hand gripped my head, massaging my hair. I could tell by the tension in his body that it was all he could do to stop himself from taking over.

"Just let me enjoy my present, Ari," I murmured as I

squeezed his dick, watching the precum as it slid down his smooth head.

"Okay," he gasped as my mouth slid over his cock, licking and sucking at the precum. "Whatever you want. It's yours. Just don't stop."

I huffed a giggle against his skin before I continued torturing him. He thrust up into my mouth and I pulled away.

"Uh, huh. I can't enjoy my present if you move."

"You mean, mean, perfect angel face," he murmured.

A thrill ran through me that I could make him like that. Desperate and needy for me. Blake. The girl who'd always felt unwanted.

"Please, fuck me," he whispered.

I licked along his head. "Like this?" I asked, my voice breathy and soft.

"More. Please give me more."

"Let's see . . . "

I took his whole head into my mouth and sucked at the slit, gobbling up more of his cum. It still amazed me that I could crave him like this. Want every drop of him inside me in whatever way I could get it.

I sucked harder and he growled. "That's so fucking good. Suck my big cock. Please. Fuck," he hissed as I began to force more of his length into my mouth.

"That's it, sunshine. Just like that," he groaned, both hands tangling in my hair, brushing against my cheeks as I tried to get deeper.

I grabbed his thighs, bracing myself as I tried different angles, trying to work his huge cock down my throat. The metal on his dick brushed against my tongue and I closed my eyes, imagining for a second how good it felt when he was inside me.

"A little more. You're taking me so well," he urged as I lowered my head further, until he was brushing against the back of my throat. I gagged against the head of his dick and he groaned again.

"Yes. Choke on my cock. Fuck. Fuck!"

His hips thrust up and I gagged again. I held him down, trying a different angle as I worked to push him past my gag reflex, into my throat.

"Yes. Fuck. Yes." His hands tightened on my head, urging me down. "Take all of it. Be my good girl and take every last fucking inch."

My eyes were watering as he thrust deeper, entering the back of my throat.

Ari suddenly stilled. "I think that since I'm such a good gift giver . . . you should give me something too."

I slid off his dick reluctantly, my tongue tracing the head as I stared at him. "Okay, what do you want?"

Instead of answering me, he flipped me around so that my pussy was positioned above his face.

Oh. He wanted that kind of present. I could definitely do that. I quivered over that first lick. His arms went around my waist, pulling me down so I had no choice but to fuck his face.

"You're going to fuck my mouth—come all over my face like a good girl," he breathed as he growled into me.

For a second, a flash of insecurity hit me. Was I too heavy on him like this? Was he thinking I was going to suffocate him? I lifted up and he yanked me down hard, forcing me back down on his face.

He nipped at my clit and I squeaked, and then the sexy bastard laughed at me. "When I say 'fuck my mouth,' I mean I don't want to breathe anything but your pussy. Got that, sunshine?"

When I didn't say anything, his hot tongue licked into me. "Are you going to be my good girl?"

"Yes sir," I moaned as I pushed down on his face, a jolt of pleasure shooting through me as his lips and tongue went to work. He speared into me with his tongue, rewarding me for my obedience.

Ari could do the one thing that no one else could. He could make me forget the outside world, forget my fucked up head. He could help me just . . . be.

I was so head over heels in love with him.

I moaned, my hips rocking as he thrust his tongue in and out of me.

My hands gripped his legs, using them as leverage as I rode his face, taking what I needed.

My legs began to shake as I chased my orgasm, and then . . . with one more lick, my muscles were tightening and I was coming all over his face.

He moaned and his licks became feverish. He held me to his mouth, lapping and sucking everything I had to offer.

Once I could breathe, I grabbed onto his dick, forcing it into my mouth.

"I want to fuck your throat, while you fuck my face again. Can I do that, baby?"

"Yes," I moaned as I licked along his shaft like it was my favorite lollipop.

Ari pulled out slowly and eased back in, his head gripping my hair as he kept me on his dick. It was a good thing he'd taken over, because there was no way for me to concentrate while his tongue and other hand were in my pussy.

He gently fucked my mouth as my hands roamed his perfect body, his pace speeding up as I got more comfortable.

"You look so fucking hot right now," he groaned as he thrust so far into my throat that I gagged.

My fingers dug into his ass, his muscles contracting under my touch as I sucked on him eagerly.

"Suck my big dick. Make me come in that hot mouth."

I whimpered as he tugged at my hair, his movements becoming rougher and harder. And then he was growling as hot cum flooded my throat and spilled out of my mouth and down my chin. I came then too, pleasure surging through me as his fingers pushed in and out of me.

I suckled on his head for a second until he was shuddering and pulling me off. And then I flopped down on top of him—completely spent.

His tongue was still softly licking at me, and we stayed like that for a few long moments until he finally shifted me around so that my head was pillowed against his chest.

I traced the tattoos on his skin as we laid there in silence.

"I'm going to take it that you fucking *loved* my present," he finally murmured and I burst into laughter, because I'd forgotten for a moment how this whole thing had started.

He started to hum the "Dick in a Box" song as my laughter continued, and he tipped up my chin so that I was staring into his dark emerald gaze.

"I love the sound of your laugh, sunshine," he murmured and my breath hitched.

"Me too," I whispered, an ache in my chest, because before Ari, I'd never laughed. And it caught me off guard every time.

He softly kissed me and one more of the cracks in my fractured heart . . . it was fixed.

———

Ari: Have you guys seen the "Dick in a Box" skit on SNL.

Lincoln: Tell me you didn't try that.

Walker: Better question is . . . did Blake like it?

Ari: That's personal information, Disney.

Lincoln: Then why did you bring it up?

Ari: I didn't bring it up. I asked if you'd seen the skit. You two just assumed I'm over here putting my dick in a box.

Lincoln: . . .

Walker: Were we wrong?

Ari: . . .

Lincoln: I hope you picked an appropriately sized box.

Ari: I know Maximus 5000's requirements, Golden Boy. I'm not going to do anything to hurt him.

Walker: I'm not sure what to say right now.

Lincoln: Me neither.

Ari: You don't need to say anything. You just need to be impressed by my creativity.

Lincoln: . . .

Walker: Okay, so I'm going to assume Blake liked it.

CHAPTER 4

LINCOLN

I parked the car near the college, waiting to pick up Monroe. It had been a long day without her, stuck in meetings with the team, and I was looking forward to getting her back in my arms.

Where she belonged.

There were still fifteen minutes until her class got out, and I sighed, staring around at the buildings while I wondered how mad she would be if I barged into the class, threw her on my shoulder, and took her home.

Probably pretty mad.

But on the other hand, I bet the make-up sex would be amazing.

I was about to call Ari to distract myself for a few more minutes from my compulsion when—

What. The. Fuck.

Monroe was walking down the sidewalk, looking like my favorite wet dream as always.

But it was the guy next to her—the one walking way too close to her and stealing glances down her shirt—that had me debating if my money could get me out of murder charges.

Monroe was gesturing and talking about something and he was hanging on her every word.

Fucker.

My fingers tightened around the steering wheel as I watched them walk.

You'd have thought that getting a ring on her finger would have made me less crazy.

But I was pretty sure there wasn't anything that would help with that. Monroe was mine. And I didn't like guys within fifty feet of her.

Sometimes I didn't like girls close by either.

I tried to count to ten before I did something insane. But then I decided . . . fuck it. And I bolted out of the car and strode towards them. "Monroe," I called out, "there you are, baby."

I reached her side and wrapped my arms around her, my lips hungrily meeting hers.

The kiss was so fucking good.

It was a kiss meant to stake my claim, to remind everyone present that she was mine and no one else's. My hand slipped down to her ass and I squeezed, wishing, not for the first time, that I could attach myself to her.

Monroe seemed momentarily surprised, but she quickly responded to my kiss. For a second, I forgot that I'd gone all caveman for a reason . . . I was just ready to get home and fuck, because I loved her so much.

I took a deep breath against her lips, a stillness spreading through my veins that only she could give me.

A throat cleared right by us and I remembered we had company.

I cast a sidelong glance at the asshole waiting by us impatiently. His eyes betrayed his emotions—his jealousy was unmistakable. His gaze had darkened, and a flicker of resentment danced in his eyes as he watched us.

I winked at him before reluctantly pulling away, snorting when I saw Monroe's gaze twinkling with a hint of amusement. She knew exactly what I was doing.

"Lincoln," she said with a smile, "meet Professor Williams. We were just discussing the story I'm writing for that creative writing contest I told you about."

Ah. *Professor Williams*. He'd been needing to have a lot of *one-on-one* meetings with my Monroe lately. But I'd thought he was a woman this whole time for some reason.

"Professor," I said, lifting my chin at him and not extending my hand for a handshake.

The Professor's demeanor was as cold as mine was, his lips curved into a subtle smirk that hinted at arrogance.

Ignoring me, the asshole addressed Monroe in a flirty tone, his voice oozing with a subtle hint of suggestiveness. "I'll see you in class, Monroe," he said, his eyes lingering on her in a way that was about to see my fist in his face.

Monroe grabbed my hand as if she could sense I was on the edge. "Thanks for the ideas, today," she said softly before turning her attention back to me.

My jaw tightened, the heat of anger surging within me. The possessiveness that was always simmering inside of me was threatening to boil over. I couldn't act rational in these situations.

Professor Williams was probably going to be fired soon.

Because "creative writing" was the last thing on that asshole's mind.

Monroe smiled up at me as we started to walk back to the car, and I immediately softened. "I've missed you, dream girl," I said, rubbing at my chest with the hand that wasn't holding hers. It was hard to explain how intense these emotions were inside of me. How I missed her even when she was away from me for one minute. If I had it my way, she'd be by my side always, stitched to me forever and ever.

I thought it was healthy that I recognized that was an insane thought.

"You've got that crazy gleam in your eyes, Mr. Daniels," Monroe smirked as I opened the door for her and helped her in, buckling her seatbelt like I always did.

"No idea what you're talking about, Mrs. Daniels," I mused, pressing another kiss against her lips because I couldn't help myself.

Monroe fiddled with Spotify, chatting about her day as I drove us home. I kept my hand on her thigh for the whole drive, unable to leave her alone—not when I was feeling like this.

We pulled into the underground garage and headed up to the penthouse. *Our* penthouse as I still had to remind her for some reason.

The elevator doors opened but I held her in place, wrapping my arms around her and pulling her towards me. "It's time for another Christmas surprise," I told her, smirking at the hitch in her breath as I pressed my hard-on into her soft stomach. "Today I'm teaching you about the wonder of Christmas lights."

"Teaching me?"

"Yes. We've already gone over the wonders of Christmas breakfast. I'm off to a great start on this whole teaching thing." My hand slipped between her legs, rubbing over the seam of her leggings like only *I* could. Only *I* knew everything about her perfect body. Only *I* knew what made her scream.

Mine.

Having decidedly lost it, I pulled her out of the elevator and down the hall where I had a Christmas Wonderland of sorts set up in the living room. There was a massive tree against the wall of windows, lit up so brightly you could probably see it from the fucking moon. Lighted garland was strewn all over the room and candles were flickering on the bookshelves and coffee table.

I watched as Monroe stared around the room in complete wonder.

"Wow," she breathed, her hand coming up to her mouth in awe. "It's gorgeous."

"Yes, it is," I murmured as I stared at her, completely entranced with her beauty. She was even more beautiful to me now than she'd been when I'd first met her.

And obviously every other guy felt that way too.

I let go of her hand and walked over towards the tree where I had pillows set up in a makeshift bed.

"Come here," I growled. I watched in pleasure as her cheeks blushed and she bit down on her bottom lip.

"Is this part of the lesson . . . *Professor*," she taunted.

Fuck me. I wasn't going to be able to control myself very long if she was going to play like this.

"Yes it is, Monroe. We have another important part of the lesson to go over," I purred.

She walked over slowly until she was standing right in front of me.

"Strip," I commanded, gratification strumming through my veins as she immediately pulled her sweater over her head, revealing an almost see-through lacy pink bra that had me almost coming in my pants.

"Fuck," I whispered, my gaze locked on her perfect tits, her rosy pink nipples peeking through the lace.

Monroe slowly pushed her leggings to the floor, until she was standing in front of me in nothing but her lingerie.

I reached out and squeezed one of her breasts. "Perfect, baby. Absolutely perfect." I breathed before I snapped her bra so it fell open, revealing her entire chest.

"Lincoln!" she huffed. "I liked that bra."

"I'll buy you another one," I said distractedly as I tore off her lacy thong next, until she was standing in front of me like I always wanted her to be.

Naked.

And mine.

"What exactly does this have to do with Christmas lights," she whispered, the pink blush spreading across her whole skin. She rubbed her legs together, and I could see the glint of her arousal on her pussy lips.

She was fucking *everything*.

I forced myself to keep with the plan and walked a few steps over towards the tree where a coil of Christmas lights was waiting. Picking them up, I went back to Monroe, who was watching me avidly.

"Hold out your wrists," I demanded in a gruff voice, satisfaction trilling through me once again as she held out her arms obediently.

Slowly, I began to wrap the lights around her wrists and up her arms. One loop went around her neck, and the rest went around her waist until she was completely covered in glittering, glimmering white Christmas lights.

"I did not see this coming," she giggled, breaking me out of my lust fog for a second.

"All part of the lesson, dream girl," I murmured as I helped her to the cushions, admiring the sight of the gleaming lights reflected off her bare skin.

"The perfect present."

Monroe

Lincoln stared down at me, a shocked look on his face like he couldn't believe what he was seeing. I also couldn't believe that I was currently naked . . . wrapped in a string of Christmas lights that were slowly blinking on and off.

I watched as he lifted his shirt, revealing golden skin and a chiseled tattooed chest that made me feral inside.

Lincoln's smirk as he removed his shirt told me he knew

exactly what I was thinking . . . and then the bastard pulled on the lights so they tightened further across my skin.

I wondered how this would have gone if he hadn't gotten jealous of Professor Williams.

Had me being tied up, always been in the plan?

Knowing Lincoln actually—yes.

My clit throbbed as I watched the shift in him, in his gaze . . . his body—the dominant, possessive, alpha-male coming out to play.

My dominant, possessive, alpha-male.

My soulmate.

"I want to be a little rough, baby," he murmured, a promise in his voice that told me delicious things were coming my way. He knelt over me and squeezed my breasts, letting out a groan as he did so.

"I keep thinking," he murmured, almost to himself. "That this need to possess you will lessen . . . Even a little bit." He shook his head. "But I think it's getting stronger."

Lincoln abruptly grabbed my bound wrists, roughly moving them over my head, securing them even more with one large hand.

His palm pressed against my chest, my heart hammering under his touch as he leaned forward, his lips grazing against my ear.

"Tonight I'm going to do everything I want to you," he said in a deep, dark voice.

I was feeling so lightheaded I was a little afraid I was going to pass out before the fun even began.

My legs rubbed together, and I could feel the trickle of moisture slipping down my thighs as I pressed into his touch.

He grabbed my legs and pulled them over his shoulders. "Everything," he said roughly, his golden gaze sending tremors across my skin.

Lincoln yanked on the lights and they tightened across my skin, especially around my neck. My breath was coming out in gasps. He moved the lights until they were in between my legs, slowly dragging them through my folds, tiny pinpricks of pain from the light bulbs feeling more like a caress under his dark gaze.

He watched them, and I watched too. The light reflected off my pink lips. He'd pulled his massive dick out of his sweatpants and was slowly jacking himself off from balls to tip as we watched the lights move across my skin.

Lincoln pushed the lights to the side and leaned forward, pressing his nose into my sex and inhaling.

"You're fucking soaked," he said with a pleased laugh. "Christmas lights for the win."

I cried out as his teeth nipped my clit, a sharp sting flashing through me.

I wasn't even embarrassed about my reaction. I'd long gotten over the fact that anything Lincoln did, I liked.

We certainly weren't going to include this scene in our Christmas card this year though—not that I was going to send any of those.

Lincoln pushed my legs further apart, dragging the flat of his tongue from ass to clit. "My favorite, favorite thing," he growled as he did it again, rougher, getting every inch of me with his tongue.

I whimpered and tried to grind against his face but he held me firm, reaching for the lights and pulling them even more, so I had no choice but to stop moving.

His tongue rimmed my opening and then pushed in as my body flushed with need. I felt feverish, pleasure licking up my spine as his nose nudged my clit. My head pushed back into the pillows and whimpers flooded out of my mouth. "Please, please, please," I begged.

His arms tightened around my legs, his biceps flexing as he

pushed harder against me, eating into my core almost desperately. His tongue speared in again and again, thrusting as deep as it could. And through it all, he was watching me, his gaze locked on my face.

My heart squeezed in my chest. I couldn't get over the way he stared at me. I'd thought that I was fine by myself all those years, not realizing I was missing part of my soul. I knew that the need I saw in his eyes was the same that he saw in mine. We were two fucked up parts of the same perfect whole.

"You look really hot right now," I gasped as the pleasure built.

He growled and sucked on my clit. Harder.

And that was all it took. My entire body clenched, my thighs quivering as an orgasm shot through me. And he drank in everything that I gave him.

Lincoln stood up and pushed down his sweatpants until he was standing there in all of his golden glory. Sometimes I lost my breath just staring at him. The lights from the Christmas tree and the garland were casting even more of a glow about him, so he looked like a fantasy.

Like this actually was all a dream.

The tips of the Christmas lights were digging into my skin, and I was a mess of sensations as he knelt down once more.

"I think I want you to look at the lights as I fuck you. Turn over." His voice was imperious . . . demanding.

I gushed at his command and he groaned as I struggled to roll over, my ass in his face as I got on my knees. It was a little difficult with my arms tied up . . .

"Look at the lights," he whispered.

And I did. I really looked.

The soft, twinkling glow bathed the room in a gentle, comforting illumination, casting a playful dance of shadows across the walls.

The other lights in the room remained off, allowing the

Christmas lights to take center stage. The fireplace crackled softly, sending tendrils of warmth into the air. As I stared at the lights, their soft flickering created a mesmerizing spectacle. They seemed to have a life of their own, a rhythmic pulse that mirrored the beating of my heart.

I realized for the first time that the room was filled with the soft strains of a holiday melody playing in the background, and my gaze traced the patterns of the lights as Lincoln's tongue dipped up my thighs, lapping up the moisture seeping from my core.

I found myself suddenly LOVING Christmas lights.

Lincoln's hand abruptly smacked down on my ass and a small orgasm pumped through me.

"Fuck. You just came," he said in an awestruck voice. His nose trailed through my folds and then he pressed a kiss to the cheek he just spanked.

I was still caught off guard from what happened, but there was a warm, fuzzy feeling spreading through my veins. Lincoln made another satisfied noise and he spread my ass cheeks. Taking more long licks from my clit all the way to my asshole. I still squirmed over that, but fuck, it felt amazing.

He slid two fingers slowly into me and I melted into the pillows, the decadent lights around me casting a comforting, magical glow as I submitted to him.

"That's it. That's my good girl." He grabbed onto my hips and ate at me ruthlessly until I was falling into another devastating orgasm.

He squeezed my asscheeks again. "So fucking perfect."

His finger slipped out of me, and was instantly replaced by his long dick. At the same time, the cord began to tighten around my neck, slowly cutting off the amount of oxygen that I could inhale.

"That's it, sweetheart. We're just going to play a little bit rougher," he soothed in a smooth voice as he rubbed his palm down my spine. He caged me in, angling his cock in and out desperately. With the oxygen deprivation, the world seemed to spin. It felt like I was in an alternate reality, the lights twinkling around me. The cord tightened more, and I gasped for breath as his fingers bit into my hips. He thrust into me hard, and that dark place inside of me, the one that only Lincoln Daniels could fill, it lapped up the mix of pleasure and pain he was giving me.

He thrusted into me, the sound of our smacking skin filling the room, combining with the Christmas music, an erotic tune I never would have imagined.

Every impact forced a cry from my lips and he leaned over and bit down where the back of my shoulder met my neck, almost savagely.

"I love you. You're mine. No one else gets to have you but me."

I couldn't respond. I was riding that fine line between consciousness and unconsciousness, my oxygen only coming in small sips as his hard body worked behind me, filling me, stretching me, reminding me who owned me.

His hand dipped between my legs and he pressed against my clit, forcing an orgasm out of me as his muscles tensed against my back.

"I love you," he chanted as he chased his own orgasm, pounding against me until I collapsed against the pillows, unable to hold myself up with the pleasure tearing through me.

The cord tightened again and I was flying, the lights swirling around me as I faded away. Pleasure was still surging across my trembling body as the sparkling Christmas lights faded to black.

I woke up on the floor, Lincoln's arm heavy across my waist. He'd unwound the lights from around me and we were cuddled up on the pillows under the Christmas tree, the fireplace flames flickering against the walls. Lincoln was tracing what I was pretty sure was his name against my back.

"How do you feel about Christmas lights now?" he murmured.

And after what had just happened . . . all I could say was . . .

"I love them."

CHAPTER 5
MONROE

I climbed onto the private plane, a huge smile on my face as I stepped inside "Grandma Airways" as Ari had dubbed my over-the-top traveling accommodations that my insanely possessive and jealous husband had set up for me.

Edna was waiting for me at the top of the steps, a warm smile on her cute, weathered face.

"Welcome aboard, darlin'," she said as she handed me a mug of hot cocoa.

Just one of the perks of traveling with the over sixty-five crowd.

I turned the corner that led to the seats, and my jaw dropped when I saw Blake, Ari's gorgeous model girlfriend, sitting in one of the leather seats, munching on a cookie as she glanced around the plane, amused. Our eyes met, and her eyebrows rose in surprise.

"Monroe?" Blake said, her voice filled with astonishment. "What are you doing here?"

I stammered. "I . . . I'm going to Lincoln's game in New York. What—"

Before we could question each other any more, our phones chimed. Almost simultaneously. We both pulled them out.

> Lincoln: Is Ari with you?

> Me: No . . . but Blake is. What's going on?

"Fuck, I love him," Blake murmured, reading the text on her phone, a faint flush to her cheeks from whatever Ari had sent her. She glanced at me. "I guess I'm going to New York this weekend with you instead of the photoshoot I thought I had scheduled." Blake's face was bemused . . . and a little anxious as she stared down at her phone. "Apparently, Ari has an in with my agent. I'll have to watch the two of them." She shook her head, biting down on her lip in deep thought.

I wasn't surprised. Knowing Lincoln and his . . . tactics . . . it would be hard to believe that Ari would be that different.

Although Ari didn't seem quite as crazy as Lincoln. Maybe I'd get the nerve to ask her about it one day. Not sure I'd ever share the whole "handcuff" incident though. I wasn't sure anyone but me and him would ever understand what had taken place then.

"Seatbelts, dearies," Edna said as she came up the row and filled my hot cocoa up to the brim even though I'd only taken a few sips.

Blake giggled again and Edna winked at her before walking up to the front to take her seat.

"You know I thought Lincoln had some kind of 'grandma fetish' when I first flew on this," Blake mentioned as she clicked on her seatbelt.

I snorted, my whole body shaking. "You did?"

She gestured around us as the plane's engines roared to life, and we started to move. "Ari didn't warn me about any of this, he just set me up for the flight and suddenly I was walking into cookies and gray hair and grandmas."

I was laughing so hard, my eyes were watering.

My phone buzzed and I glanced down.

> Lincoln: What are you laughing so hard about?

That only made me laugh harder, an edge of insanity in my voice because of course he had his app engaged so he could watch me through my phone. The sound must not be working though, and I'm sure that was driving him insane.

Insaner than he already was.

I'd never known that I was crazy, not until I discovered the other half of my soul and realized it.

> Me: Blake thought you had a grandma fetish.

> Lincoln: Fucking Ari. I told him to warn her!

I snorted again.

> Me: How exactly does Ari warn his girl that you're kind of crazy?

> Me: Correction. Take out the "kind of," and leave just "crazy."

> Lincoln: You're just asking me to spank you, aren't you?

> Me: Yes, Daddy.

> Lincoln: . . .

> Me: 😌

Lincoln: Thanks for making me hard. On the plane. With my teammates.

Me: Glad to be of service.

Lincoln: Just get your pretty ass to NYC.

Me: Say please.

Lincoln: Grrrr.

Lincoln: Love you, dream girl.

I glanced up, relieved to see that Blake wasn't staring at me like I was crazy or rude because I'd drifted off into Lincoln land—somewhere I found myself most of the time.

She was staring at her own phone, probably texting Ari by the soft smile on her face.

I had slowly been getting to know Blake in the times Lincoln and Ari could steal away from their teams. She was gorgeous. One of the prettiest girls I'd ever seen in my life, in fact. And I would have loved her just for the fact that Ari loved her. In the last few months though, I'd found her to be one of the sweetest, most caring women I'd ever met. She also had a charming sense of humor that somehow went perfectly with Ari's goofiness.

I didn't have a lot of friends. And I didn't really have time for them, since Lincoln and I basically existed in our own little world. But we did have our little crew that was like family to us. And Blake had now joined Ari in that crew.

Blake and I chatted about my classes and some campaigns she'd done, along with how the guys' season was going.

It had been really hard for Lincoln not having Ari on the team. But he seemed really confident that Ari was going to "lock it up" and be back in Dallas with Blake next season.

And yes, I had asked what "lock it up" meant in that context . . . since you could never be sure with Lincoln.

His answer had been vague.

Staring at Blake though, whatever Ari was doing, he was doing it well. She'd had a haunted look in her eyes when I'd met her that first night in the bar. And now, just a few months later, that look was almost gone.

It was another reason that I felt so bonded to her . . . I'd had that haunted look in my eyes before Lincoln as well.

My phone buzzed.

> Lincoln: I fucking miss you.

> Me: Me too.

It was a crazy thing that you could miss someone like this. Lincoln and I didn't get tired of each other. Sometimes I thought maybe we should take a minute away from each other . . . that it would be healthy.

But Lincoln always quickly convinced me why that wasn't a good idea.

Mabel came then with the tea service. I was pretty sure that most flights—even private—did not come with tea service. But Mabel and Edna were very insistent on it every flight.

"It was good for the soul," or something like that.

Instead of her usual sweater and skirt uniform, Mabel was wearing a Christmas cat sweater today that said "Meowy Christmas—I'm Feline Festive." A quick glance at Blake and she was just as amused as I was judging by the wide grin on her face as she stared at Mabel.

"We've whipped up some sugar cookies to go with this apple cinnamon tea, darlins'," she told us as she poured the steaming tea into Christmas-themed china she'd pulled off a tea cart.

Edna slipped past Mabel to hand us a tray of decorated

Christmas cookies. The cookies themselves were an assortment of shapes, meticulously frosted with vibrant red and green icing, forming intricate designs of snowflakes, candy canes, and jolly Santas. The sugary coating glistened on top.

And my mouth was already watering.

For a second a memory filtered in.

I was seven years old, and it was Christmas time at my elementary school. Mrs. Rawlings had handed out these wonderful sugar cookies, each one shaped like a beautiful Christmas tree with red and green frosting. It felt like a little piece of holiday magic in my hand.

As the other kids excitedly nibbled on their cookies, I decided to save mine. It was going to be a special treat for my mom when I got home. I gently wrapped the cookie in a napkin and tucked it into my tiny backpack, careful not to let it break.

When I finally walked through the door of our small, sad apartment, I was bursting with anticipation. My mom was there, but she was in a state I had seen all too often, lost in her own world with the smell of alcohol heavy in the air.

"Mom," I had whispered, tiptoeing closer, my heart pounding with excitement, "I brought you a Christmas cookie."

She turned to me, her eyes unfocused and bleary, and for a moment, I wasn't sure if she even knew I was there. But then, with a sudden, reckless gesture, she snatched the cookie from my hand, her laugh more like a cruel, mocking cackle.

With a swift, heart-wrenching motion, she threw the beautiful cookie to the ground. It shattered into a million crumbs, its festive shape obliterated, and my heart shattered with it.

My hand moved away from the tray, my appetite suddenly gone.

"You know, I made this one especially for you, sweetheart," Mabel said sweetly, reaching over and grabbing a Christmas tree of all things from the tray Edna was holding. She placed it in my hand and I stared at the red and green icing on top for a few seconds before lifting it up to my mouth.

Everything else Lincoln had me do this Christmas had worked like magic to erase the darkness of my past.

Maybe this would too.

I took a bite of the cookie. The sweet, buttery flavor filled my mouth, and it was like a little piece of heaven. Mabel was chattering away about how it was an old family recipe that she had decided to share with Edna.

Edna, never one to miss an opportunity to snark, couldn't resist. "Oh, yes," she said with a sly grin, "But I've made a few improvements to the recipe. That's why it's so much better now."

Blake couldn't help but burst into laughter as the women started arguing over the cookie recipe.

I couldn't help but smile too, munching away at the cookie. It was delicious, and the love and laughter in the cabin was contagious. In that moment, surrounded by these women . . . I suddenly felt a whole lot better.

Maybe sugar cookies didn't have to be ruined either.

CHAPTER 6
BLAKE

As the plane began its descent into New York City, I couldn't tear my gaze away from the window, my emotions in turmoil. The city sprawled beneath me, a vast, glittering expanse of lights and memories, a place that held both the promise of excitement and the weight of painful history.

I hadn't set foot in this city since I had run away—run away from the Shepfields, from Clark, and from a life that had become suffocating. The memories that resided here were a tangled web of joy and sorrow, and I wasn't sure how to unravel them.

I leaned my forehead against the cool glass, feeling a mixture of anxiety and anticipation gnawing at my insides. Ari had surprised me with this trip because I'd told him the other week that there was no place like New York for Christmas—that it was the only thing about New York I missed. He was trying to give me whatever I wanted, just like he always did.

But the past still lingered, like a shadow that refused to fade. The city's skyline, so iconic and breathtaking, felt like a constant reminder of everything I had left behind. I could almost hear the echoes of conversations, the laughter, and the tears that had once filled the streets.

The plane continued its descent, bringing me closer to the city that had shaped me in so many ways—not for the better. The familiar landmarks came into view—the towering skyscrapers, the bustling streets, and the twinkling lights of Times Square.

I took a deep breath, trying to push aside the apprehension that clung to me like a second skin.

The wheels of the plane touched down, and Monroe bounced around in her seat excitedly. I pretended to be excited too. I didn't want to ruin the trip for her, or for anyone.

I made a silent promise to myself that I would embrace this opportunity. Ari was my superman. I was pretty sure that with him by my side, I could conquer anything.

Even the ghosts of my past.

We said goodbye to Edna and Mabel and stepped off the plane. There was a sleek, black limousine waiting for us just a short walk away.

The limo gleamed in the afternoon sun, its polished exterior reflecting the vibrant cityscape around us. The chauffeur, a woman of course, dressed in a crisp black suit, stood by the open door, ready to greet us with a warm smile.

We climbed into the plush interior of the limo, sinking into the soft leather seats that cradled us in comfort. The scent of leather and polished wood filled the air, adding to the sense of opulence. Tinted windows shielded us from the bustling world outside, creating a cocoon of privacy in the midst of the city's chaos.

"I'm never going to get used to this," Monroe said in awe, accepting the glasses of sparkling cider that the driver handed to her before she closed the door. Ari had told me she didn't drink very much, if at all, so the cider made sense. I was grateful mine was champagne, though. I needed some liquid courage at the moment.

"Get used to what?"

"This," she laughed, gesturing around her. "I'm in a limo . . . after just getting off a private plane. Drinking from a fancy glass. On my way to watch my rich hockey player husband play in front of thousands. It's . . . surreal." The end of her sentence came out as a whisper.

I scooted closer and wrapped an arm around her. "It's freaking awesome, right? How lucky are we?"

She grinned. "Yeah. It is *freaking* awesome."

We sipped our drinks as we drove through Manhattan. A million memories in my head.

The towering skyscrapers reached for the sky, their glass façades reflecting the sunlight in a dazzling display.

Yellow taxis weaved in and out of traffic, while pedestrians hurried along the sidewalks, lost in their own world. We passed by the Empire State Building and Central Park, all bathed in the golden light of late afternoon.

There was a different energy here than in L.A., a constant vibrant, pulsating heartbeat that hit me in my gut.

And then I saw it. The Metropolitan Museum.

The sight of it hit me like a tidal wave. The memories of that day—of running down those steps—came rushing back, and it was almost incomprehensible how much my life had changed since that moment.

It was incredible how a single decision, one word spoken in a moment of clarity and desperation, had completely reshaped my world.

As I gazed at the Met, I couldn't help but wonder about the alternate reality where I had said yes to Clark. Would I even be alive right now? Or would I have drowned already, consumed by the world I'd been trapped in?

"Blake . . . are you alright?" Monroe whispered, her green eyes wide and soulful as she stared at me.

I gave her a smile, but I knew it felt flat. "There's a lot of memories here. A lot of demons so to speak."

She nodded, looking thoughtful. "I know all about demons. I'm conquering a few of my own this season . . . all the seasons." Monroe squeezed my hand and my heart thumped.

It was nice to have a friend.

———

The limo pulled to the back of the arena where Lincoln was playing, and the driver got out to open the door for us. Before she could get to the door, it was yanked open and there was Ari. He immediately reached in and plucked me out, swinging me around in his arms and burying his face in my neck. His body shuddered like he'd been in withdrawal and I was just the hit he needed.

"Fuck. I missed you. I missed you. I missed you," he growled, keeping me plastered against him as he smacked a kiss against my lips.

"Hi," I smiled against his mouth. "I missed you too." It didn't feel as hard to be vulnerable with him anymore, not when he was giving me all of him. Every day. "But I'm confused why you didn't just fly with us."

He scoffed, and his arms tightened around me once more before he reluctantly slid me down his body. Belatedly, I realized Walker was standing a few steps away, his hands in his pocket, looking adorably awkward as he pretended not to watch us. "You can thank 'Golden Boy' for that," he said with a sigh as he waved to Monroe behind me.

"Oh boy. What did my husband do now?" Monroe said with mock exasperation as she walked up next to us.

"Linc threatened 'Little Ari' with bodily harm if he rode on the plane with Monroe without him," Walker supplied helpfully.

My jaw dropped. But Monroe . . . she didn't seem shocked at all.

Ari's whole body was shaking against me.

"And that would be why he never answered my text asking why he was wondering if you were on the plane with me."

"I sent him a photoshopped picture of me sitting on the plane next to you." Ari was bent over now, unable to control himself because he was laughing so hard. "He literally called me fifty million times. And then he called Mabel and Edna just to make sure."

Walker was shaking his head at Ari . . . or Lincoln. Both called for a head shake at the moment.

Ari straightened, wiping at his eyes. "It's too good. I can literally torture him for the rest of our lives about Monroe. You're the gift that keeps on giving, bestie," he said, patting Monroe on the head like she was a puppy.

Monroe rolled her eyes, scrunching up her nose adorably. "Let's go inside before he comes out looking for me." With the way she was marching towards the arena though, I think she was just as antsy to see Lincoln.

Ari grabbed my hand again and dragged me against him.

"You know I would have been on that plane with you, Golden Boy aside, but I figured you and Monroe might want some girl time. Did you have a good time?"

"I really did," I told him, melting against him. "Monroe's a keeper."

"Mmmh, you're a keeper," he murmured, pressing a kiss on my lips that had me contemplating if we could sneak in a quickie somewhere.

A throat cleared and we both glanced behind us to see Walker standing there. "Can we not make me feel like the thirdest wheel of all third wheels," he huffed.

Ari smacked my ass. "Disney, I can't keep my hands off of her. I'm addicted. #sorrynotsorry."

Walker sighed and shook his head. "I did sign up for this."

Ari then smacked *him* on the ass. "Get in there, Disney. And find yourself a soulmate."

Walker's face fell. "Yeah. Yeah."

But he didn't look excited about it.

———

Monroe

"Please, please, please," Ari was pleading with me. He was currently on his knees in the hallway outside of where our seats were located, trying to convince me to wear his jersey for at least one of the periods.

"Do you have a death wish?" I drawled as Blake and Walker huffed out laughs.

"Possibly. But that's besides the point. I need this. Walker needs this. Your bestie Blake needs this."

Walker put up his hands in front of him. "I want it on the record that I am *not* a part of this."

Ari rolled his eyes so dramatically, they almost disappeared. "Of course, you don't want to be a part of this, Disney, you little simp."

"I just don't want Lincoln mad at me."

"Sigh. Fine. I will tell Lincoln you weren't a part of this."

"How are you going to do that if you're dead?" quipped Blake.

"Exactly," I nodded seriously.

"Monroe. This is all I want for Christmas," Ari pleaded, somehow still on his knees.

There were flocks of people staring at us and I was starting to get embarrassed.

"For the next five years!" he said louder, causing even more people to stare.

"Fine," I hissed. "Just get up!"

Ari had a smug expression on his face as he slid smoothly to his feet.

"Thank you."

"We are not *besties* anymore," I told him.

"Please. I'm lovable. You and Lincoln love me." He pulled Blake into his side. "Tell them I'm loveable."

"You are so loveable," she purred, hearts in her eyes.

So cute.

"I'm right here," groaned Walker.

"We're well aware, bro," Ari snarked, blowing him a kiss.

"Let's go in," I said with a sigh as I slipped on Ari's old Dallas jersey.

We walked into the stands, making our way down to the second row where our seats were located.

A crisp, almost metallic aroma of freshly cut ice hung in the air. It mingled with the earthy undertones of the wooden boards that encased the rink. The sounds of skates slicing through the ice greeted us—sharp, rhythmic hisses that reverberated through the arena. The murmur of the crowd filled the air, a constant hum of anticipation and excitement. The voices of fans, young and old, blended together in a chorus of cheers and chatter.

It was amazing how it all had become so familiar to me, this world I'd never imagined before.

Lincoln's gaze locked with mine and butterflies cycled through me. The urge to reach out and touch him was a beating drum in my chest. Judging by the way he was staring at me—he felt the same way.

I'd missed him even in the few hours we'd been apart.

I loved him so much it hurt.

And I didn't think that was ever going to change.

He pointed at me and then raised his hands . . . in a heart sign.

Like he had in every game since that first time.

I squirmed in my seat and Blake shot me a knowing glance from beside me.

Warmups finished and Lincoln lined up at center ice, his stick tapping in a rhythmic cadence, a fierceness in his eyes that was . . . freaking hot. The arena's lights gleamed brightly over-head, casting a spotlight on the pristine ice surface.

The ref dropped the puck, and in an instant, the game was underway. The clash of sticks, the sharp scrape of blades against ice, and the unmistakable thud of body checks echoed through the arena, creating a pulse of energy that surged through the crowd.

The play unfolded with breathtaking speed and precision. Players weaved through the neutral zone, passing the puck with pinpoint accuracy. Shots were fired on the goals, each one accompanied by a collective intake of breath from the crowd. The goaltenders made spectacular saves, and the crowd groaned and cheered with every near-miss, every breakaway, and every thunderous hit along the boards.

We were at the end of the first period when Lincoln finally managed to break through the opposing team's defense. He deftly maneuvered the puck, his stick slicing through the air, and then, with a flick of his wrist, Lincoln released the puck.

It soared through the air, a perfectly executed shot that left no doubt in anyone's mind.

The puck was going in.

It slipped past the goaltender's defenses and into the back of the net.

The crowd erupted in cheers, and I jumped to my feet, my heart pounding with excitement and pride for my man.

"Suck it, Conroe," Walker yelled, and Ari glanced at him, impressed.

"Disney, I didn't know you had it in you."

"I hate that guy. He shared a video online last year before we played each other that was just a montage of goals scored against me. Fucking douchebag," he griped as he lifted his shirt.

Ari followed suit with a big grin on his face and I turned to stare at what was painted on their chests.

"We Love You" was on Ari's chest, and "Golden Boy" was on Walker's.

I snorted as the women in the crowd went absolutely wild as the cameras panned on Walker's and Ari's perfect chests and abs and they appeared on the Jumbotron.

The crowd suddenly hushed abruptly though, and I glanced at the ice to see if something had happened. Only to see Lincoln.

He had torn off his jersey and was standing there in his hockey pads, his arms folded across his chest.

His face was very unamused as he stared at me, and I froze.

"Looks like Linc just noticed your jersey," Blake whisper-yelled next to me.

"I think you're right," I responded, unable to take my eyes away from Lincoln.

He skated over to the glass in front of us and banged on it, releasing a tirade filled with a bunch of f-bombs. His glance went to Ari who had the biggest grin I'd ever seen on his face, and he made a slicing motion across his neck.

"I will kill you," he mouthed.

I sighed. "Great. Now you're going to get him kicked out of the NHL because he just threatened you on national television."

"Nah. We're giving the people a show. And the big guys always like a show," he snorted as we continued to watch Lincoln lose it.

Lincoln skated over to the bench and threw his jersey to an assistant, pointing to me as he did so. I stood there, in utter mortification as the assistant scrambled up the stairs like his ass was on fire and handed me a jersey.

"Please put this on before I lose my job," he begged as a bead of sweat fell down his forehead that was out of place in the cold arena.

Lincoln had somehow come up with another jersey and was slipping it on as he skated over to watch and make sure I put it on.

I fumbled for a moment as I hastily removed Ari's jersey from over my long sleeve top, and slipped into Lincoln's. The moment the fabric settled on my skin, the grateful assistant scurried back to the bench.

The crowd's cheers erupted as soon as the jersey was on, and apparently Ari was right . . . they did love a show, because they were even louder than they'd been before.

Lincoln nodded and mouthed an "I love you," before he skated back to start play.

"If Lincoln doesn't kill you, I'm going to kill you," I hissed at Ari with a hand over my mouth to hide my words since the Jumbotron was *still* on us.

Ari pulled Blake into him and laughed. "Please. I just made sure you'll get the best sex of your life. I'm a hero."

"Make sure he knows I had nothing to do with it!" Walker inserted in a panicked voice.

And we all laughed.

CHAPTER 7

LINCOLN

I was playing with her.

But it was torturing us both.

It had taken all of my control to play it cool for the rest of the game.

And now as we headed to dinner.

My hand was on her thigh as I pretended to listen to the story Ari was telling, my finger slowly stroking higher inch by inch.

Her body was tense as she sat next to me, her gaze constantly flicking towards me, wondering when I was going to make my move.

I had to torture her . . . at least a little bit.

I'd once promised her if she ever wore another man's jersey . . . I would kill him.

Unfortunately in this case . . . I loved the fucker.

Or maybe I could just control myself from killing Ari because I knew how obsessed he was with Blake.

More obsessed than she could even comprehend.

As if he could sense I was thinking about him, the bastard winked at me while he continued on with his story.

I couldn't kill him. But when we played next I would probably maim him . . . at least a little bit.

I played with a piece of her hair, picturing myself wrapping it
around my fist as I fucked her from behind. I shifted in my seat
because my dick was all of a sudden hard like a rock.

"So, where are we going?" Blake asked as Ari slid her from
her seat onto his lap.

"Mmmh, what's your favorite fancy dinner in New York,
sunshine?" he murmured, nuzzling into her hair.

It was still a little weird to see him like that. How he acted
with Blake was completely different than how he'd acted with
anyone in the past. They'd been nothing, and he'd treated him
like that—cold and distant so they didn't get the wrong idea. He
treated Blake like . . . she was everything.

I could understand the feeling.

"Yo Disney, can you get some "Christmas Tree Farm" playing? I'm in the mood for a little . . . Tay Tay."

Walker was manning the music for the drive, but so far, he
was mostly just playing all of Ari's favorite songs.

"What about 'Tis The Damn Season?'" Walker asked,
scrolling through some songs.

"Is that a Christmas song?" asked Blake. "It's kind of
depressing."

"It's the greatest Christmas song there is," said Walker,
aghast.

"Okayyyy," I drawled slowly. "Tell me you're not getting
laid, without telling me you're not getting laid."

Walker literally growled at me before slapping a hand across
his mouth. "Sorry! I didn't mean that," he said frantically.

There was a moment of silence as Ms. Swift began to play her
depressing "Christmas" song . . . and then we all burst into
laughter.

Just then, the St. Regis popped into view and Blake gasped
before staring at Ari with big moon eyes. Monroe stared out the

window interestedly, probably wondering what the big deal was. My girl was still pretty naive about expensive things, and it was going to be a blast giving her this experience tonight.

I helped Monroe out of the limo, shooting the hovering doorman a look when I saw him staring at her legs. He blanched and quickly glanced away. I didn't blame him for wanting to look, but it didn't change that I wasn't going to allow it to happen.

When I stared down at Monroe—*my Monroe*—my breath caught in my throat. She was wearing a tight, crimson dress that clung to her every curve, accentuating the graceful lines of her body. Her long, silky hair cascaded down her back, framing her delicate features. My fingers itched to rip that dress off and it—combined with the jersey incident—was making me feel a little feral at the moment.

"Down boy," Ari muttered to me as he passed by.

I growled at him and he snorted.

"Nick Soto," I muttered under my breath, forcing myself to think of the carrot topped troll who played in LA., to make sure my hard dick didn't scare the maître d'.

But then Monroe smiled up at me, and I was fucked.

"Did you just say Soto?" Walker asked, staring at me confused.

I rubbed a hand down my face, wanting to hit him with a hockey stick. "Don't worry about it, Disney. You must have misheard me."

"No, I think I heard that, too," said Ari innocently. "You fantasizing about Soto again, golden boy?"

"I hate you both," I growled as I flipped them off with the hand that wasn't holding Monroe. Their laughter followed us all the way through the grand lobby as we made our way to Astor Court, the hotel's famous dining establishment.

As we entered the restaurant, a hostess greeted us with a flirty smile. I sighed and glared at her until she got the point that I wasn't interested. Monroe's face was bemused when I glanced down at her, but she didn't get upset anymore when women came onto me.

She knew I was all in, that no one existed but her.

I had her name inked on my dick for fuck's sake.

She owned me.

We were led to our table. The ambiance was impeccable as it always was, with crisp white linens, gleaming silverware, and crystal stemware that caught the candlelight.

"This place is nice," Monroe whispered as I pushed her chair in.

"Wait until you taste the food," I whispered back.

We ordered their holiday three-course dinner, complete with butter-poached lobster risotto, dry-aged prime rib, and pan-roasted wild striped bass—and yes, I'd gotten that description from the menu.

Ari was even quiet for once, shoveling the delicious food into his mouth because it was so fucking good.

Monroe's smile lit up the room, especially when they brought out their famous Buche Ispahan yule log and Grand Marnier panettone bread pudding. I didn't eat much of the dessert though . . .

Because the part of the night I was *hungry* for was about to start.

———

Monroe

He was teasing me.

Or maybe torturing me was the right word. I was in a gorgeous hotel, eating food that almost rivaled Mrs. Bentley's . . . and I could barely concentrate on any of it.

The soft glow of candlelight played upon his perfect features, casting shadows across his face that made him look even more of an otherworldly creature—a god among men.

I'd finally realized he was up to something, and I was more than willing to play along.

His fingers, warm and teasing, brushed lightly against my skin, tracing a tantalizing path along my arm, as I tried to taste my lobster bisque.

I squirmed in my seat, struggling to keep my composure, and taste my damn dinner. But I was starting to crave something else.

Who needed food when you had Lincoln Daniels?

I took a sip of my Diet Coke, my lips touching the glass just as his fingers grazed my cheek. I shivered into my glass, my eyes locking with his in a silent dare.

Lincoln continued his seductive assault, his fingers now drifting lower, playing with a strand of my hair. He wound it around his fingers, tugging ever so slightly, and I couldn't suppress the soft gasp that escaped my lips. His eyes gleamed at me wickedly.

"Behave," I mouthed, but he just winked at me.

His touch ventured further as dinner progressed, his hand finding its way to my thigh beneath the table. His fingers danced along the fabric of my dress, inching upward in a maddeningly slow ascent. Each caress was deliberate, sending sparks cascading across my skin.

I feigned interest in the story Walker was telling, but my attention was solely on Lincoln's touch. He leaned in, his breath warm against my ear, and whispered, "What do you think, Monroe? Should we try the prime rib?"

His voice sent a shiver down my spine, and I had to bite my lower lip to stifle a moan. All I could do was nod.

Somehow no one else at the table seemed to notice what was happening.

Thank fuck.

Lincoln chuckled softly, his fingers now tracing the curve of my inner thigh. My pulse quickened, and I couldn't help but let out a soft, longing sigh.

As the evening progressed, Lincoln's little game only intensified. He fed me bites of our exquisite meal, his fingers brushing against my lips as I savored the flavors. Each bite was decadent, but it was his touch that left me craving more.

By the time dinner was almost over, my nerves were shot.

I forced myself to take some bites of the bread pudding, my foot tapping in an anxious rhythm, wondering how much longer Lincoln was going to make me wait.

Finally he stood up, grabbing some folded bills out of his wallet and throwing them on the table.

"We've got to go," he said through gritted teeth, desperation finally leaking through.

Ari smirked at us. "What's the rush? I was thinking we should get some drinks at the bar after this."

"We'll have to pass," Lincoln answered, grabbing my hand and all but dragging me out of my seat and away from the table.

"Bye," I called out feebly as our three friends cackled at us.

Lincoln didn't say a word until we were in the elevator. And then all he did was crowd me into a corner, his hand gently grabbing my throat as he leaned in close.

"Mine," he growled.

And all I could do was nod, my breath coming out in gasps.

It was so true.

———

"Take it off," he ordered the second we'd gotten into the hotel room he'd booked for the night.

"What?" I asked, a little out of sorts from that elevator ride where he'd pushed me against the mirrored wall and finger-fucked me.

And hadn't let me come.

"Take that fucking dress off that's been torturing me all night . . . before I rip it off."

"Oh," I murmured, immediately pulling on the dress because I really liked it and didn't want it ruined. Although staring at the feral glint in Lincoln's gaze . . . it would be worth it.

I slid the dress off, enjoying the look of pain on his face as he watched me like his life depended on it. I hadn't worn a bra or underwear because I hadn't wanted lines. So once the dress was off, I was completely naked.

I tossed it onto a nearby chair. I went to step out of my heels, but he held up a hand. "Keep those on."

"Sir, yes, sir," I whispered, and his eyes *burned* for me.

"Now on your knees," he said roughly.

I kept his gaze as I fell to my knees, as gracefully as I could in four-inch heels.

"Good girl," he murmured, taking a slow step towards me. "Now put this on." He threw me a jersey that I hadn't noticed him grab. I lifted the fabric, smirking when I saw that it was obviously his.

"Oh you think that's funny, do you?" There was an edge of madness in his voice that sent shivers down my spine.

"It wasn't my idea . . . " I said lightly.

"Obviously I knew that. Because we've had this conversation before, haven't we, Monroe? About whose jersey you're allowed to wear?"

I nodded as he took another step towards me, sliding off his suit coat and slowly unbuttoning his dress shirt.

"I want your words," he pressed.

"Yes," I whispered, pulling the jersey over my head. Before I could pull it on all the way, he caught the fabric, holding my hands above my head.

"I like this view," he purred, and a second later I felt his warm mouth on my nipples, suckling and biting them until I was writhing against his face.

He moved away abruptly and I cried out. Lincoln pulled the jersey the rest of the way down until it pooled to the floor.

"Please," I murmured.

"Please what?" he asked mockingly.

I squeezed my eyes closed and rubbed my legs together, trying to ease the ache.

"Please fuck me," I finally whispered.

"I think it's time for the next part of your education for one of the great things about Christmas, actually," he answered.

I bit down on my lip and shivered at the darkness in his gaze. "And what's that?"

"The color red."

Lincoln pulled a red ribbon from his pocket and dangled it in front of my face. "Hands behind your back."

I hesitantly obeyed him, reaching my hands behind me, and he swiftly tied my wrists together with the ribbon. My breasts jutted out, and I could just imagine how obscene I looked at the moment.

As if he could sense my thoughts, he spent a moment kneading and massaging my breasts before he cursed.

"Up," he growled, making no move to help me as I struggled to my feet.

Lincoln went to one of the big velvet armchairs that sat by the floor-to-ceiling windows that looked out at the city, and he sat down in it with the ease of a king who had claimed his throne. His posture was relaxed, and he sprawled out, commanding the space around him.

He leaned back, stretching his long legs out in front of him.

The room seemed to bend to his presence, as if the very furniture had been arranged to accommodate his aura of dominance. His gaze, sharp and focused, surveyed the surroundings with a hint of amusement, as though he were privy to a secret that the rest of the world had yet to discover.

He was magnetic, captivating, and it was moments like this that I couldn't believe he was mine.

"Come here."

I walked unsteadily towards him immediately, stopping hesitantly in front of him.

"On my lap."

Oh, that sounded fun.

But as I went to straddle him, he instead pulled me forward until my chest was on his legs and I was bent over him.

Lincoln rubbed my bare ass and I finally understood what he'd meant by "red" . . .

"I think you need a little reminder about whose jersey you wear, dream girl," he said in a thick voice that told me just how much this was affecting him. His dick told the rest of the story, hard and thick against my chest. "Now count."

There was sharp pain as his hand suddenly slapped down on my bare cheek and I squeaked in surprise, thrashing against his legs. His arm braced over me, halting my movements. "What number was that?"

"One," I whispered, a flood of heat dripping from my core.

He soothed the sore spot. "That's my sweet girl."

Lincoln's hand came down again.

"Two!"

Slap. Slap. Slap.

His hand cracked down on my ass again and again and I did my best to count.

But my insides clenched with every sharp sting of his hand, and confusing pleasure was building in my core.

Lincoln's fingers traced through my folds and he swore viciously. "This is turning you on. You like it," he murmured delightedly.

All I could do was moan against his lap.

"You're not allowed to come, Monroe," he ordered sternly, and I whimpered in response.

"Three more. I think a perfect *thirteen* should do it. Don't you think?" he asked wickedly.

Of course he would pick that number.

Another spank. "Are you ever going to wear another man's jersey again?" he taunted.

Crack.

"No," I whispered as need surged inside me.

Two more spanks and I was coming, my cries filling the room as an orgasm burst through me, my vision going in and out from the extreme pleasure.

I laid there on his lap as I came down, my breath coming out in gasps.

"Red is such a perfect color," he murmured as he caressed my skin. "But you're a naughty girl, coming when you weren't supposed to."

"I'm sorry," I murmured.

"I think you need to make it up to me, Monroe."

"And how am I going to do that?"

"Get on your knees and suck my big cock," he growled.

I was on the edge of coming *again*, just from thinking about doing that.

He helped me off his lap and I pushed between his legs, gazing up at him as he pulled out his dick and leaned back in the chair.

I stared at it hungrily, my gaze devouring the sight of my name on his beautiful cock. I'd never get over the crazy, unhinged perfection of it.

My tongue darted out and licked at his tip, sucking in the flavor of him—my favorite. I didn't play any more though, I was too turned on. My lips locked around him and I feasted, taking him as deep as I could.

His groans filled the room and minutes later, his cock

twitched, and my mouth was filled with bursts of warm, thick cum that I drank down desperately.

Lincoln gathered me in his arms, pulling me into his lap. His mouth slammed against mine and we both groaned as our teeth and tongues tangled with each other. He stood up and carried us over to the bed, undoing my wrists before he laid me down gently and wrapped his body around mine.

"How do you like Christmas colors now?" he murmured contentedly as his hands stroked down my skin.

"I love them," I whispered as I snuggled against him. And seconds later, I was asleep.

And visions of sugarplums might have just danced in my head.

CHAPTER 8

Ari: Anyone have a Santa hat I could borrow?

Lincoln: Do you really think I carry a Santa hat with me?

Walker: But also . . . what do you need it for?

Ari: Does that mean you have one? You do, don't you?

Walker: I mean . . . maybe.

Lincoln: Why exactly do you have a Santa hat with you?

Walker: . . .

Ari: . . .

Ari: Okay . . . but just checking . . . has it been anywhere near your dick yet?

Walker: What? No!

Ari: Phew.

Lincoln: This is weird, even for the two of you.

Ari: I'll be up in five to get it.

Walker: Wait! Are you planning for it to be anywhere near your dick?

Ari: . . .

Lincoln: . . .

Walker: Yeah, you can keep it.

———

Blake
New York City was more than ever, a place of contrasts for me—filled with memories both beautiful and painful. But on this crisp December morning, I was determined to embrace the magic of the holiday season with my friends and Ari, making new memories that would replace the old.

Our day started with a visit to the iconic Rockefeller Center. The towering Christmas tree, adorned with thousands of shimmering lights and ornaments, still took my breath away. The ice rink below was a hive of activity, with skaters of all ages twirling and gliding to the tunes of classic holiday songs.

Of course the guys couldn't resist the lure of the ice, and soon, we were all lacing up our skates, ready to take on the rink.

Ari held me tight as we glided across the ice, his strong arms holding me up since I was a terrible skater.

"I think you're getting better," Ari offered as I almost took us both out.

I giggled and grabbed onto him tighter. "You think?"

"Definitely. We managed not to take out that kindergarten class. Major improvement."

We watched as Lincoln hoisted Monroe up on his shoulders and casually skated across the ice like it was nothing.

"Show-off," Ari muttered before scooping me up into his arms.

"What are you doing?" I squeaked as he suddenly jumped in the air and did a 360 degree spin with me in his arms, landing smoothly on the ice.

"Just making sure *Golden Boy* knows who's truly the excellent skater in the group," he replied cheerfully as Lincoln scowled at us.

Just then Walker whizzed by, somehow managing *two* spins in the air before he landed. The skaters around him cheered.

"Walker wins," I quipped as Ari growled at me.

"No cheering for Disney."

"I didn't cheer."

"You smiled at him!"

"Okayyyy," I said sarcastically, and he winked at me.

Once the guys were done showing off, we headed over to the bustling holiday market in Union Square. Stalls were set up as far as the eye could see, offering an array of handmade crafts, festive ornaments, and delicious treats. The air was filled with the scent of freshly roasted chestnuts and hot cider, and the atmosphere was vibrant and merry.

We strolled through the market, sipping on steaming cups of cocoa and admiring the handcrafted goods. I couldn't help but pick out a few unique ornaments to adorn our Christmas tree back in Los Angeles, a reminder of this special day in the city.

"Too bad there isn't a tattooed dick ornament," muttered Ari as he and Lincoln watched Monroe and I pick out ornaments.

"Tattooed dick?" squeaked Walker, giving them the side-eye.

Ari nodded seriously. "In honor of Linc."

"You tattooed your dick!" Walker whisper-yelled, and an angry mother covered her daughter's ears as she hurried them away.

"Want to tell all of New York?" drawled Lincoln, not sounding particularly upset about the idea of that.

I turned my attention back to Monroe and the ornaments . . . not wanting to imagine Lincoln's dick.

"What exactly does he have tattooed on there?" I asked Monroe, not able to stop myself.

"My name," she said nonchalantly as she examined an Empire State Building ornament. She side-eyed me after a moment and then we both erupted in peals of laughter.

A second later, tattooed arms were wrapping around her and Lincoln was nuzzling into her hair.

I jumped when Ari pulled me into his chest. "What's so funny over here, sunshine?"

Monroe and I locked eyes again. "Nothing," she squeaked, and we burst into laughter again.

Lincoln growled, but there was a gentle smile on his lips. A quick glance over at Walker, and he just looked uncomfortable.

I giggled again.

"Love the sound of your laugh, sweetheart," Ari murmured to me, brushing a kiss against my neck. "Are you having fun?"

I turned in his arms so I could stare up at him. "The best," I whispered, amazed at how good he was at replacing memories of my past with good ones.

He stared down at me, something I couldn't read in his gaze. "Good," he finally said, stroking his hand down my cheek.

After we paid for our ornaments, we made our way to Bryant Park, where a winter wonderland had been created with an ice-skating rink and rows of quaint holiday shops. The giant Christmas tree in the center of the park glittered with multicolored lights, and the scene was straight out of a holiday postcard.

Lunch found us at a charming little café in the West Village, where I introduced the group to the best hot chocolate in the world. After taking one sip, Ari somehow convinced the shop owner to ship us a few pounds of his homemade mix.

As the sun began to set, we headed to Fifth Avenue, where the holiday window displays were out in full force. The storefronts of famous department stores had been transformed into elaborate scenes of holiday enchantment. We took our time wandering from window to window.

There was one final stop to make before dinner—the observation deck of the Empire State Building.

We stood there at the railing, Ari's arms wrapped around me, taking in the magnificent view of the city that never slept.

"I think you're a little bit magical, Ari Lancaster," I whispered as we stared at the city skyline, with its sparkling lights and skyscrapers reaching for the heavens.

"Yeah, sunshine? And why's that?"

I turned in his arms, like I had earlier, thinking that the view from this angle was much better than the one behind me.

"I didn't think I could ever come back here . . . and like it."

"Baby steps," he murmured, staring down at me intensely with that stunning emerald green gaze of his.

"What?"

"I said I would make you happy. And happiness is a process. One that I intend to succeed at *Every. Fucking. Day.*"

My breath hitched and wetness slid down my cheek.

"Is that alright, sweetheart?" he whispered so tenderly, my heart literally ached.

"Perfectly alright," I answered softly.

As we gazed out over the city, I felt a deep sense of gratitude. Gratitude for the chance at happiness it felt like Ari was giving me after a lifetime of tears, for the friends who had become my family, and for the magic of the holiday season that surrounded us.

————

Ari

We'd just gotten back to the hotel room after the most Christmassy day I could recall . . . but it wasn't over yet.

I had a little surprise of my own planned for my girl.

"Wait right here for a second," I told her with a mischievous grin before disappearing into the bathroom. I swiftly changed into a pair of red Santa bottoms I'd gotten the hotel to drum up for me, leaving my upper body gloriously shirtless to display my toned abs.

With Walker's Santa hat perched jauntily on my head, I opened the door that led back into the bedroom, and leaned against the doorway, striking my most inviting pose.

"Want to sit on Santa's lap?" I asked, my voice laced with playful suggestiveness.

Blake's reaction was priceless. Her mouth opened and closed as if she were searching for words, her eyes dancing with a mixture of amusement and surprise. I'd caught her completely off guard . . . understandably. Her gaze dragged up and down my body, getting caught on my abs . . . exactly my intention.

"I hear if you sit on a bearded man's lap, you get what you want," I teased.

She pretended to think about it for a moment, tapping her finger on her chin. "But you don't have a beard."

I gasped. "Hmmm," I mused, "I am feeling a little *bare* down here." I motioned theatrically to my chin, feigning seriousness.

She burst into laughter, and I grinned.

I may not have been Santa Claus, but I was *certainly* ready to grant her wishes.

I stalked towards her, falling to my knees and abruptly cutting off her laughter. "I wonder what I could . . . wear instead?" I slowly pulled down her leggings and underwear. "What do you think?"

Blake was staring at me, a flush creeping up her chest. "I can think of something."

I admired her pretty pink folds, already glistening with arousal. I'd have to watch my back—Santa obviously turned her on.

"Tell me, sunshine. Have you been a good girl this year?" I gave her one long lick that had both of us groaning.

"Yes, yes, yes," she chanted.

"So you're not on the . . . *naughty* list?"

"No. Definitely not."

"Damn," I said, pushing away from her perfect pussy.

"What?!"

"Only naughty girls get tongue-fucked by Santa," I told her seriously.

She stared at me for a second. "Oh, I've been really naughty," she amended desperately. "The naughtiest. I've been a bad, bad girl . . . "

I smiled up at her brightly. "Oh good. I was hoping you'd say that."

I licked into her again, dragging my tongue from her clit . . . to her ass, somewhere I was desperate to fuck. "You taste even better than cookies," I told her, my voice muffled as my tongue rimmed the opening of her core. It was getting harder to roleplay. I just wanted to fuck her.

"That's good, Santa," she whimpered as I speared into her.

Not sure I liked another man's name coming from her lips . . .

My nose nudged her clit and I licked and sucked desperately. She needed to orgasm so I could get my dick into her sweet cunt. It was a need at this point.

"So good," she cried as I used my fingers to fuck in and out of her so I could concentrate on her clit.

Thanks to the fact that I knew her body better than she did, I had her coming a minute later . . .

I jumped to my feet and held out my hand, making a big show of licking my lips so I could catch every bit of her delicious taste.

"Ready to sit on Santa's lap?" I asked, walking backwards as I pulled her with me.

"Only if you promise me more . . . presents," she said.

I grinned. "Definitely."

A second later, I was plopped down in one of the high-backed chairs, tearing at my belt so I could whip out my dick.

Dammit . . . I should have put a bell on the tip. That would have been way more festive.

I forgot all about that when she straddled my lap. My hands automatically went to her hips, holding her against me, trying not to come just from the feel of her wet pussy against my cock.

"Santa's going to fuck you now, sweetheart," I growled as I lifted her up and then slammed her onto my dick.

Her head fell back, a gasp falling from her lips, and I was right there with her. Nothing felt as good as my cock buried deep inside her.

It was where I belonged.

"That's it, baby. Let Santa fill you up."

A half-hearted snort passed from her lips, but I wasn't going to let her laugh at Santa.

I fisted a hand in her hair, tugging her face towards me as I claimed her lips in a hungry kiss—licking, sucking, and biting at her mouth so she definitely wasn't laughing at "Ole Saint Nick" anymore.

Using my other hand, I lifted her as I fucked up into her, a violent, savage hunger overtaking me.

"Fuck," I growled as her dark blue eyes held me captive, like they always did.

Blake wasn't content to go along for the ride though . . . she lifted her hips on her own and started to ride me, bouncing up and down in my lap frantically.

I desperately tore at the tanktop she'd been wearing under the sweater she'd already taken off, ripping it in half so I could get to her perfect tits. I sucked the rosy peaks into my mouth, sucking and biting gently at them as she continued to fuck herself on my dick.

"Fuck, fuck, fuck."

Sleighbells, gingerbread . . . why the fuck wasn't anything helping! I was about to come and it was way too quick.

"I need you to come," I gasped frantically, taking over and slamming her down on me. "Right the fuck now."

"What's wrong, Santa?" she teased, her voice thick with lust.

"Blake," I growled. "Fucking come."

A few more bounces on my dick and I finally felt her clenching around me. I couldn't stop myself from following her over the edge, ecstatic pleasure rushing through me as I pumped my cum into her.

I buried my face into her neck, groaning because it felt so fucking good. Every time with her was the very best.

"Ho, Ho, Ho," I muttered when I could finally actually speak.

There was a beat of silence, and then her body was shaking against me as she laughed.

I huffed, because the movement was too much against my sensitive dick.

"Give me a second, and Santa will show you what's in his bag of toys," I tossed out.

She lifted my face from her neck and stared at me, a beautiful smile on her fucking perfect face.

"Merry Christmas, Santa," she whispered.

And fuck, I was suddenly ready to go again.

CHAPTER 9
MONROE

I was officially a big fan of Christmas.

Which maybe shouldn't have shocked me.

If there was one thing that was true about Lincoln, when he set his sights on something . . . it was going to happen.

And it *had* happened.

For the rest of the month after we'd gotten back from New York City, Lincoln had continued his quest to make me like all things Christmas. We'd gone through most of the Christmas classics—my favorite being Jim Carrey's version of *How the Grinch Stole Christmas*.

Made even better by the orgasm he'd given me at the halfway mark.

I still wasn't sure about the fact that "You're a mean one, Mr. Grinch" was now an aphrodisiac . . .

In between his hockey games, we'd gone to The Nutcracker at Bass Hall, gone ice skating again at The Galleria, and drank hot chocolate as we drove around looking at Christmas displays.

And then there was this morning: Christmas Day, when I'd woken up to what felt like a million presents under the tree.

I'd started crying. Absolutely weeping. Because I'd never had a tree with presents under it my entire life.

I hadn't even wanted anything, it was just the sight of it. For some reason, it healed even more of the cracks inside me.

"I have one more present for you," he'd murmured to me after I'd spent an hour opening up an entire store's worth of gifts—if that store was a mix of Neiman Marcus, Tiffany's, and Dior.

"What is it?" I asked. "I can't think of anything you didn't buy me at this point, Lincoln."

"Just open it, dream girl," he ordered in that bossy way of his.

With trembling hands I ripped open the pretty packaging.

And then I was sobbing again, because in my hands . . .

Was an angel ornament.

"Lincoln," I whispered, my hand trembling as I touched it.

"There isn't a part of you I'm not going to heal. It's the only thing I want in life, to make you happier than you've ever been," he told me seriously, his golden gaze piercing into me.

I carefully put the angel on the tree, and turned towards him, my palms softly holding his cheeks.

"Mission accomplished," I told him as his lips crashed against mine.

And then neither of us spoke . . . for a long, long time.

―――

We'd just gotten back from his Christmas Day game and were in the kitchen eating some of Ms. Bentley's tamales, when the familiar ding of the elevator echoed through the penthouse.

"Oh! I have one more surprise," Lincoln said as he led me down the hallway to its polished metal doors. I was a little distracted by the sight of his ass in his gray sweatpants.

My own personal thirst trap.

We turned the corner right as the elevator doors slid open, and my eyes widened in surprise. There, standing before us, was Bill.

But this was unlike any version of Bill I had ever seen. He was dressed in a well-fitted suit, a stark departure from his usual rugged—and dirty—appearance.

Beside him stood a small group of people, each holding a lyric sheet and wearing expressions of holiday cheer. They broke into a joyful chorus of Christmas carols, their voices harmonizing in perfect unity. Bill, who I had always known to be zany and unpredictable, was now leading them with confidence.

"Deck the halls with boughs of holly, fa-la-la-la-la, la-la-la-la," they sang, their voices filling the elevator with festive warmth.

I stood there with my mouth open in astonishment, as I watched Bill, with a twinkle in his eye, continue to lead the group in song. His voice, usually affected by a fake British accent, was now filled with genuine merriment. He looked at me with a playful wink, clearly relishing the moment.

And then . . . Lincoln joined in. His deep voice blending as they sang "Jingle Bells." I hurriedly pulled out my phone and recorded it.

Because a memory wasn't enough for this moment.

The carolers concluded their serenade with a resounding "Merry Christmas!" and then all of them left but Bill.

"Merry Christmas, little duck," he said, smelling much better than he usually did as I gave him a hug.

"Merry Christmas," I murmured back in a choked voice, my gaze locked on Lincoln.

As we headed with Bill towards the kitchen to feed him some tamales, I caught sight of the glowing Christmas tree in the living room, and the angel sparkling under the lights.

Merry Pucking Christmas indeed . . .

EPILOGUE

WALKER

A few months later . . .

The tension on the ice was thick as the first period ended. I stood between the pipes, taking in every detail, every sound . . . every movement on the ice. Adrenaline was pulsing through me. I'd stopped every puck that came my way so far, and the anticipation was building as we inched closer to securing our playoff spot.

Hopefully Lincoln was coming through for us in his game.

Not that I doubted him for a second.

That man was a god.

Ari shot me a thumbs up as he skated by and I readied myself for the next period to begin. "Good fucking job, Disney. Circle of trust behavior for sure."

I rolled my eyes, but I was feeling pretty proud of myself.

But then, amid the cacophony of cheers and shouts from the crowd, there was a distinct, piercing voice that cut through the noise. A girl's voice, loud and unabashed, telling me that I . . . sucked. It happened all the fucking time obviously . . . but something had me turning my head.

And there she was, standing on the other side of the glass, her eyes locked onto mine.

Mine.

I felt lightheaded as I stared at her, the world rearranging around me until all I could see . . . all I could feel . . . was her.

Time seemed to stand still as I blew her a playful kiss, watching in awe as her gorgeous face screwed up in disgust, gold-flicked eyes unaware that she'd just changed my fucking world.

The buzzer sounded and I reluctantly dragged my gaze away from hers and towards the action happening on the other side of the ice, a new life goal in place.

To do whatever it takes to make that girl fucking mine.

BONUS SCENE

Want more Lincoln, Monroe, Ari, and Walker? Come hang out in C.R.'s Fated Realm to get access to exclusive bonus scenes!

Get it here: https://www.facebook.com/groups/C.R.Fated Realm

SNEAK PREVIEW

Turn the page to keep reading—*The Pucking Wrong Man* available in paperback Fall 2024!

CHAPTER 1

ANASTASIA

DALLAS

KNIGHTS

I opened my eyes slowly, the harsh lights of the hospital room blinding me for a moment before my vision cleared.

Where was I?

The room swam, and I winced, quickly closing my eyes again and taking a deep breath.

My entire body hurt.

Okay, I could do this, I told myself, opening my eyes just a crack this time so I could get used to the light.

Finally able to open my eyes wide enough, my gaze immediately fell on my leg . . . which was encased in a giant cast from my ankle to my thigh.

What had happened?

It took a moment, but then it all came back, my own personal horror story playing out in a macabre technicolor in my head. My father lunging at me, the sharp crack in my leg, and pain like I'd never experienced before.

My chest tightened as I stared at the cast, my breath coming in shallow gasps as an icy hand seemed to clutch at my heart.

Was I ever going to be able to dance again?

The edges of my vision were darkening, a panic attack fully setting in. And then a hand landed gently on my arm, causing me to jump in surprise. I turned my head to see . . . Michael? He was standing next to the bed, his too-perfect smile immediately making bile clog my throat. What was he doing here?

"Hey, hey, it's okay," he said, his voice unnervingly calm. "You're going to be alright, Ana."

I shook my head frantically, tears stinging my eyes as I tried to make sense of what was happening. Michael was the *last* person I wanted to see. What was going on?

"Why are you here?" I managed to choke out, my voice barely above a whisper.

But Michael just smiled that same too many teeth—psychopath smile, his eyes shining with a glint that made me want to jump off the bed and run down the hallway as fast as I could . . . to anywhere but here. "You've been injured badly. I just wanted to be here for you," he answered, his voice almost . . . mocking, like he knew something I didn't. "I didn't want you to be alone."

I still didn't understand what was going on. How had I gotten to the hospital? Where was my dad? Why would Michael, of all people, be here?

He reached down as I watched . . . and pushed my foot to the side.

I screamed.

It was like I was being torn apart, the pain radiating up my leg, through every fiber of my being.

The door burst open, and a team of doctors rushed in, their voices a blur of urgency as they worked to calm me down. I felt hands on my shoulders, holding me in place as they injected something into my IV, the world around me growing hazy and distant.

I tried to tell them what he'd done, but I couldn't form words around the fog of pain and medication. Michael's face hovered above me, his eyes filled with *terrifying* satisfaction. Darkness closed in, and I couldn't help but wonder if one terrible thing had become far worse.

"Goodnight, little bunny," he whispered as I lost consciousness.

———

Things hadn't improved when I woke up, although the pain was at least tolerable enough that I'd stopped screaming.

Michael was still there, hovering close to me. Most of the time his hand was on my shoulder in what would have looked like a comforting gesture to anyone else—but to me was definitely a threat. I'd spent the last year shying away from his touch, only for him to touch me constantly for the past hour.

Nurses had been in and out, but none of them had caught my desperate looks. I was going to have to say something—but would anyone believe me?

A sharp rap on the door jolted me in the bed, the sound echoing through the sterile hospital room like a gunshot. The medicine they'd given me still had me off my game, and I jumped at any sudden sound or movement.

The door swung open without me saying they could come in, revealing two imposing figures in police uniforms and a stern-looking woman in a stiff skirt suit. Their presence immediately filled the room with an oppressive weight, and I shrunk back instinctively, my eyes wide with apprehension as they entered. A knot of dread coiled in my stomach as I watched them.

"Hello there, Anastasia," the taller officer greeted me with a somber nod, his voice surprisingly gentle despite his imposing figure. "I'm Officer Rodriguez, and this is Officer Thompson. We're here to talk to you."

The woman in the skirt suit offered a strained smile as she stepped forward next. "And I'm Ms. Jenkins, your caseworker. How are you feeling, dear?" She was trying to sound kind, but she wasn't very good at it. I also hadn't missed how she had called herself *my* caseworker. What was that going to mean for me?

I swallowed hard, my throat suddenly dry as I struggled to find my voice. "Everything hurts," I mumbled, my gaze flickering nervously between the three of them. "What's going on?"

Officer Rodriguez exchanged a glance with Officer Thompson before he spoke again. "Do you remember what happened to you?" he asked, his warm brown eyes filled with sympathy.

I shrunk further into the bed, scared to answer them, because I'd heard horror stories at school of what happened to kids when they were taken from their parents.

Worse things than what I had experienced with my dad.

"Anastasia, it's okay," Officer Rodriguez soothed.

"My dad was drunk. He thought I was someone else and he—he hurt me," I finally whispered, my gaze focusing on my leg. No one had explained yet how bad the injury was. I needed to know.

"Thank you for being brave and telling us. He's been arrested, but we needed to hear you say that so we can keep him from ever hurting you again," the other officer said, his voice gravelly and authoritative. "What he did, Anastasia, he won't be getting out of prison anytime soon."

Even at my age, I obviously knew you couldn't just hurt your kids as bad as my father had hurt me without consequences. But it still felt as though the ground had been ripped from beneath me, leaving me flailing in uncertainty. "What does that mean for me?" I managed to choke out, my voice barely above a whisper.

The officers exchanged a look. "That's where I come in," Ms. Jenkins interjected, her tone falsely cheerful as she stepped forward. "You'll be staying with the Carvers for the time being. You won't even have to switch schools! They're a *lovely* family, and I'm sure you'll be very comfortable there."

"What?" I gasped as Michael's fingers dug into me. I glanced up at him, flinching at the smirk playing on his lips. My stomach started to hurt as reality set in.

I froze, terror seeping under my skin, and Michael's fingers tightened, but I shook my shoulder, and he finally let go, probably wanting to play nice in front of these people.

The caseworker's friendly mask dropped when she saw the expression on my face. "Anastasia!" she said, sounding appalled. "I don't think you understand the severity of the situation. You should be over the moon that we don't have to put you in the system! The Carvers are absolute angels for taking you in. We're just lucky that they are already on the approved state list to be foster parents. There are a million children who would give anything to have such a generous offer. You should be *grateful!*" Shaking her head, her face changed back into a picture-perfect look of concern.

"The medicine and your injuries are obviously confusing you. We should let you get some rest, and we can discuss this later, when you're not in so much pain." Sighing as if she was trying to pray for patience to deal with me, she gestured to the officers. "Let's let her rest. The poor dear needs time to heal."

The officers nodded.

"We'll have some more questions to ask later," Officer Rodriguez told me. I nodded numbly, and then he and his partner left the room.

"Michael, dear. Why don't we go talk to your parents and leave Anastasia to get some rest," Ms. Jenkins simpered. She was obviously already under Michael's gross spell, showing she was a terrible judge of character—a trait probably needed for a caseworker.

"Of course." Michael smirked, giving my shoulder a squeeze for good measure before he headed for the door. "I'll see you later, *sis.*" He threw the words over his shoulder, his smile reminding me of the Joker's.

And then I was alone. Nothing but numb silence surrounding me.

A tear slipped down my cheek, and I angrily brushed it away.

But it was a useless effort, because there were a million more tears that came after that.

Another knock sounded on the door, this one soft and non threatening.

"Come in," I called in a hoarse voice, rubbing at my face frantically just in case it was the caseworker . . . or Michael. I didn't want either of them to see me cry.

But it wasn't them. Thankfully. Instead, a kind-looking woman with a neat bun and a white coat slowly opened the door and popped her head in. Unlike with the caseworker, the doctor's concerned look seemed genuine. I wasn't sure how I could even know that—it was probably wishful thinking. But the soft smile she was giving me still somehow made me feel calmer.

"Hello, Anastasia," she greeted me softly. "May I sit?"

I blinked at her question, and then nodded numbly, watching as she pulled a chair up to my hospital bed.

"I'm Dr. Patel. I'm in charge of the team helping you while you're with us."

I returned her smile weakly, feeling a sense of relief wash over me at her calming presence. "Hi, Dr. Patel," I replied, my voice barely above a whisper.

She settled into the chair beside me, her expression gentle. "May I?" she asked again, nodding her head at the IV in my arm. I liked that she kept asking my permission, even if it was just a formality.

I nodded, and she carefully checked where it was protruding from my arm before sitting back in her chair.

"I'm afraid you suffered a concussion from the . . . incident," she said, her words careful. "You also have a bruised spleen, which is why you're feeling so sore."

I nodded like I understood what all that meant. There was only one real injury I was concerned about, though. "And my leg?" I asked, my voice trembling as I stared at the cast.

"Your leg," she began, her voice softening even further, "it's broken in two places. You had two surgeries while you were out—" My head jerked up at that news. She held up a hand like that would calm me down. "We had to set the bones back in place. They had broken through the skin, and it was an emergency situation."

I was feeling lightheaded at that news. I remembered the snap and the sharp pain . . . and then the numbness that had spread through my limbs.

"The good news," Dr. Patel continued, "is that you shouldn't need to have any more surgeries unless the hardware gives you trouble."

I nodded slowly, my mind reeling as I tried to process everything she was telling me. A concussion, a bruised spleen, a broken leg. That was—a lot.

"Dr. Patel, how long do you think it will take for my leg to heal?" I asked. "When can I get back to my dance classes?"

Her brow furrowed slightly, and she hesitated before answering, her expression somber. "Well, Anastasia, injuries like yours are quite serious," she began carefully. "Usually, people with these kinds of injuries are lucky if all that's left when it heals is a limp."

My heart dropped, and it was suddenly hard to breathe.

"I can't dance anymore?" My voice was high-pitched and squeaky, and the lightheadedness was getting worse. This wasn't happening. I was going to wake up and this was all going to be nothing but a bad dream. I had to dance. I had to. I was either dreaming or she was lying.

I wanted to scream or cry or rage because I would be alright with anything else being taken away from me.

Anything but losing the ability to dance.

I was faintly aware of Dr. Patel's hand on my arm. "Anastasia, *usually* doesn't mean *always*," she said gently, her voice infused with reassurance. "And things could be different for you, if you follow directions and work hard at physical therapy and anything else we ask you to do." She paused. "You also have youth on your side. Things could end up better than if this injury had happened later on."

I nodded, her words giving me a spark of hope that I was going to hold on to for dear life.

I would do whatever she said. I *was* going to dance again.

The door opened then, and Michael popped his head in, not bothering to knock. I tensed up.

"Can I help you, young man?" Dr. Patel asked.

"Just checking on Anastasia. My family will be taking care of her," he said, his face the epitome of concern.

Dr. Patel clapped her hands together. "Oh, that's wonderful. I'm so glad she's going to have a support system."

That numbness, the one I'd experienced as I lay on the floor of my room, it was spreading through me again.

But this time, I embraced it.

I stayed numb when they discharged me a week later, wheeling me out to Michael's smiling parents who shared the same watery-eyed cold stare as their son.

I stayed numb when they locked me in my new room.

I stayed numb when they made me ask permission for any food I wanted to eat in their home.

I stayed numb when I had two more surgeries on my leg, and an infection set in that made me sick for weeks.

But I gritted my teeth when I took my first step in physical therapy, and it hurt so bad I felt like I might die.

I forced myself to walk, and then to walk even farther, and then to run.

And when it was finally time, I forced myself . . . to dance.

Mrs. Bentley's Christmas Pancakes

SERVINGS: 4

INGREDIENTS

2 CUPS SWEETENED FLAKED COCONUT

PANCAKES

4 CUPS FLOUR
1 TEASPOON SALT
1/2 CUP BUTTER MELTED (PLUS EXTRA FOR COOKING)
1 1/2 TABLESPOONS BAKING POWDER
1/4 CUP SUGAR
3 EGGS
3 CUPS BUTTERMILK
2 TEASPOONS VANILLA

TOPPINGS

1/2 CUP MACADAMIA NUTS CHOPPED

COCONUT SYRUP

1 - 14 OUNCE CAN COCONUT MILK NOT LITE
1/2 CUP SUGAR
2 TABLESPOONS LIGHT KARO SYRUP
PINCH OF SALT

INSTRUCTIONS

PREHEAT OVEN TO 250 DEGREES. SPREAD COCONUT ON LARGE BAKING SHEET AND TOAST FOR ABOUT 18-20 MINUTES OR UNTIL GOLDEN. ANOTHER OPTION IS TO PLACE OVEN TO BROIL SETTING. TOAST COCONUT OVER BROIL FOR 1-2 MINUTES OR UNTIL GOLDEN. WATCH CAREFULLY AS IT CAN BURN QUICKLY UNDER THE BROIL SETTING.

TO MAKE PANCAKES:

IN LARGE BOWL, STIR TOGETHER FLOUR, BAKING POWDER AND SALT. STIR IN MELTED BUTTER, SUGAR, EGGS, BUTTERMILK AND VANILLA.

HEAT LARGE SKILLET OR GRIDDLE OVER MEDIUM-LOW HEAT. TEST FOR READINESS BY SPRINKLING SOME WATER ON PAN AND IF IT SPATTERS OFF THE GRIDDLE, IT'S HOT ENOUGH. COAT WITH BUTTER OR SPRAY WITH NONSTICK COOKING SPRAY.

USING A 1/2 CUP, POUR PANCAKE BATTER ONTO PAN OR SKILLET. GENEROUSLY SPRINKLE WITH TOASTED COCONUT. WHEN BUBBLES APPEAR ON TOP OF PANCAKE, FLIP TO COOK THE OTHER SIDE. WATCH CAREFULLY AS PANCAKES CAN BROWN QUICKLY. KEEP IT AT A LOWER HEAT TO ENSURE THAT THE INSIDE GETS COOKED THROUGH WITHOUT THE OUTSIDE GETTING TOO BROWN. SERVE WARM.

TO MAKE COCONUT SYRUP:

PLACE CANNED COCONUT MILK, SUGAR, AND KARO SYRUP IN MEDIUM SAUCEPAN OVER MEDIUM HEAT. WHISK TOGETHER AND COOK FOR 8-10 MINUTES OR UNTIL IT STARTS TO SIMMER. ONCE IT STARTS TO SIMMER AND THICKEN, REMOVE FROM HEAT AND SERVE.

TOP PANCAKES WITH COCONUT SYRUP, MACADAMIA NUTS, AND REMAINING TOASTED COCONUT.

ACKNOWLEDGMENTS

You guys asked for more . . . and I made sure it happened for you. I love these characters so much. They are far more than a story about obsessed hockey psychos. I hope you burn and cry and laugh with these characters like I do.

Love you guys . . . and Merry Christmas!

I'm so thankful to the following people: Crystal, Blaire; you're always there for me on a moment's notice. Your encouragement lifts me up. I adore you. Patti; thank you for stepping in, reading, and helping make them shine! And to you, the readers who make all my dreams come true. It is a privilege to be able to write these words for you, and I will *never* take you for granted.

ABOUT C.R. JANE

A Texas girl living in Utah now, C.R. Jane is a, mother, lawyer, and now author. Her stories have been floating around in her head for years, and it has been a relief to finally get them down on paper. Jane is a huge Dallas Cowboys fan and primarily listens to Taylor Swift and hip hop (. . . don't lie and say you don't, too.)

Her love of reading started when she was three, and it only made sense that she would start to create her own worlds, since she was always getting lost in others'.

Jane likes heroines who have to grow in order to become badasses, happy endings, and swoonworthy, devoted, (and hot) male characters. If this sounds like you, I'm pretty sure we'll be friends.

Visit her C.R.'s Fated Realm Facebook page to get updates, and sign up for her newsletter at **www.crjanebooks.com** to stay updated on new releases, find out random facts about her, and get access to different points of view from her characters.

Podium

DISCOVER MORE
STORIES UNBOUND

PodiumEntertainment.com

Printed in the USA
CPSIA information can be obtained
at www.ICGtesting.com
JSHW080503200924
70118JS00002B/2